D1169930

101 DETECTIVES

101 DETECTIVES

STORIES

Ivan Vladislavić

LOS ANGELES · HIGH WYCOMBE

First published in southern Africa in 2015 by
Umuzi, an imprint of Penguin Random House South Africa (Pty) Ltd.

First published in this edition in 2015 by
And Other Stories
Los Angeles – High Wycombe
www.andotherstories.org

Copyright © Ivan Vladislavić 2015

All rights reserved. No part of this publication may be reproduced, stored in a retrieval system, or transported in any form by any means (electronic, mechanical, photocopying, recording or otherwise), without the prior written permission of the publisher of this book.

The right of Ivan Vladislavić to be identified as Author of *101 Detectives: Stories* has been asserted by him in accordance with the Copyright, Designs and Patents Act 1988.

This book is a work of fiction. Any resemblance to actual persons, living or dead, events or places is entirely coincidental.

ISBN: 9781908276568
eBook ISBN: 9781908276575

Editor: Michael Titlestad; proofreader: Beth Lindop;
typesetter: Nazli Jacobs; cover design: Hannah Naughton.

A catalogue record for this book is available from the British Library.

In memory of
Chris van Wyk

Contents

The Fugu-Eaters

'Hey, Klopper, what's a gonad?'

Klopper did not answer.

Tetrodotoxin. Bate turned the word over in his wounded mouth. It was found in the gonads of the fugu fish and a grain of it was enough to kill you. It paralysed the nervous system, shutting down your organs one by one, until you died a horrible death.

'Listen here,' he said. '*The fugu fish is twenty-seven times more deadly than the green mamba.* Incredible.'

The back of Klopper's head bristled. Bate could imagine the morose expression on his face.

Bate was sitting on the bed reading a copy of the *Reader's Digest*, which he'd carried away from his dentist's waiting room the day before. He'd been halfway through the article on fugu fish when the nurse summoned him to the chair and so he'd slipped the magazine into his jacket pocket. This morning, when he put the jacket on again, there it was. A label stuck to the dog-eared cover read: 'Please do not remove from the waiting room.'

Klopper was at the window of the hotel room, looking out into the street. He was sitting the wrong way round on a chair, with his folded arms leaning on the backrest and his chin propped on one wrist. Glancing down through the gap between the frame of his glasses and his cheek he saw the digits on his watch flashing. Eleven hundred hours, eleven hundred hours.

Bate shifted on the mattress so that he could rest his shoulders against the headboard.

'Don't put your shoes on the bedspread,' Klopper said, without looking round.

'Get off my case.' And Bate thought: He's got eyes in the back of his head – but how do they see through that stuff? In the nape of Klopper's neck was a sludge of bristly grey hair, like iron filings in grease. Maybe his glasses had little mirrors in the corners, like those spymaster specs they used to advertise in the comics.

'Is he coming?'

'I told you already, he won't pitch until this afternoon.'

'What's the point of watching all day then?'

Klopper's neck bulged. 'Did you go to school or what?'

Bate stuck the tip of his tongue in the hole at the back of his mouth where his wisdom tooth had been. It was no longer bleeding, but it tasted of blood.

'Mr Bate,' Dr Borkholder had said, 'it doesn't look good. These wisdoms will have to go. But a clever chap like you won't even miss them. Some of the others are also too far gone . . .'

'It's sergeant, if you don't mind.'

'You haven't been flossing, sergeant. This molar is holding on by a thread.'

'Do I need a filling?'

'I'm afraid it's too late for that. You should have come to me ten years ago. There's not a lot I can do now. I might be able to save a couple at the side here and these two' – tapping on them with a silver rod – 'but most of them will have to go. To give you a better idea . . .'

He opened a drawer in a cabinet and took out a plastic model of the human jaw. It was a gory-looking thing, with gleaming white fangs jutting from inflamed gums.

'Forget it!' Bate said, trying to sit up in the chair. Bloody sadist. Any excuse to use the pliers. The whole profession was a racket. He jerked the armrest up and a tray of instruments clattered to the floor. The dentist gaped behind his plastic visor. Bate would have punched his lights out, but the nurse came running.

'Sergeant Bate' – bitch had been eavesdropping – 'please, you must get a grip on yourself. Or we'll . . .'

Or we'll what? Call the police?

He calmed down. Even made an apology of sorts.

'How would *you* feel if he told you your gums were shot?'

'You're putting words in my mouth,' Dr Borkholder protested.

Then the nurse prepared the syringe and they gave him an injection and pulled out a wisdom tooth, bottom, left. He felt no pain. It should rather have hurt, he thought afterwards, then the sound might have been less sickening, the splintering in his head like a door being battered down as the dentist worked the pliers back and forth, twisting the roots out of the bone.

'So what's this crap about fish?'

'Page 76.'

It was Bate's turn at the window. He was sitting back to front in the same pose as Klopper, sitting that way to feel what it felt like to be Klopper. He heard Klopper leafing behind him. All ears, that was the secret.

A little yellow card, with the proposed date of Bate's next extraction scribbled on the back of it, fell out of the magazine. Klopper put it in his pocket and began to read aloud:

'*The flesh of the fugu fish contains one of the deadliest toxins found in nature, and yet it is eaten everywhere in Japan. Some gourmets regard it as the ultimate gastronomic experience.* Trust the bloody Japs. *In 1986, two hundred and sixty people died from eating fugu, but many cases go unreported, and the actual number of fatalities is much higher. What is the appeal of this deadly delicacy?*'

'The appeal,' said Bate, who had already read the next paragraph, 'is (a) it tastes amazing, and (b) it makes you irresistible to chicks.'

The bedsprings creaked. Bate pricked up his ears and tried to picture what Klopper was up to. A soft thud. Klopper dropping the magazine on the floor. More creaking. Klopper making himself comfortable.

'Take your shoes off the bed,' Bate said, without looking round.

'Piss off.'

He glanced over his shoulder and saw Klopper's shoes at attention on the carpet, his toes squirming in his socks.

The fire had been the Captain's idea. When Klopper thought about it afterwards, that was always the first thing that came into his mind. The two of them had brought the evidence to the farm on the back of the bakkie, wrapped in plastic and covered with a groundsheet and a load of firewood, just to be safe. The plan was to bury it in the veld behind the windbreak, but the wood gave the Captain the idea for the fire. 'What's buried can always be dug up again,' he said. 'But what goes up in smoke is gone for good.'

One of the constables was waiting for them at the house. It was Voetjie, the one with the limp. The Captain told him to offload half the wood at the end of the stoep, where they usually made the braai, and call them when he was finished. Then they took the cooler bag out of the cab and went to wait inside.

They were drinking beer at the kitchen table when Voetjie came to the door to say it was done. You'd think he was a bloody servant, Klopper thought, you'd never say he was one of us.

Voetjie climbed on the back of the bakkie and they drove out towards the bluegums. Then it occurred to the Captain that a fire might look suspicious out there and so they circled back to the dam. From down in the dip they could see the roof of the farmhouse on the ridge in the distance, glaring like a shard of mirror in the dusk.

When they untied the groundsheet Voetjie didn't bat an eyelid, and Klopper guessed that he'd already sniffed out what was concealed underneath it. The two of them dragged the bundle off the tailgate, stretched it out on the ground next to an overgrown irrigation ditch, and piled logs over it. It was like building a campfire, Klopper thought.

The Captain himself sloshed diesel over the pyre. At the last minute, he bent down, jabbed a forefinger through the plastic and tore it open. He gazed through the gash as if he was trying to read something in the dark. Then he stepped back and struck a match.

Klopper kept watch while Bate ate his lunch at the dressing table on a sheet of newspaper. 'When we leave,' Klopper said, 'I don't want a crumb left behind to show that we were here.' All Bate could manage was ice cream. The Sputnik Café downstairs was out of tubs, which would have been more convenient, so he had to settle for a Neapolitan slab. He ate it from left to right, which happened to be the order of his preference – chocolate, strawberry, vanilla. He spooned it into the right-hand side of his mouth, away from the tender hole, but it made his teeth ache.

The *Reader's Digest* lay open beside him, pinned flat by an ashtray, and he read as he ate, glancing up at himself from time to time in the dressing-table mirror.

'This fugu stuff is so dangerous you have to get a licence to cook it.'

'Come off it.'

'It says here: *Only qualified chefs are allowed to prepare fugu dishes. The training is long and arduous, and at the end of it the candidates have to pass a stringent examination. Identifying and excising the poisonous parts of the fish is an exact science. But mistakes still happen, even in the best establishments.*'

When the ice cream was finished they changed places and Klopper ate his Russians and chips. The sausages had burst open into gnarled shapes in the cooking oil. Deep-fried organ meat, he thought, something a Jap might like. He wiped them in the smear of tomato sauce congealing on the waxed paper. He looked at Bate in the mirror while he chewed.

'I suppose you still hungry?'

'I could do with a steak.'

'I should of got you some of that fish.'

'Fugu.'

'And chips, no salt and vinegar.'

The burning had taken longer than they anticipated. Klopper and the Captain sat on a ruined wall, drinking beer and watching the light fade on the water, or squatted in the flickering shadows, tending the fire. Klopper had imagined it would be over in half an hour, that they would be back at the house in time to watch *Due South* on television. But at seven o'clock it was still burning fiercely. When they ran out of logs the blaze died down at last, and then a jumble of angular shapes became visible in the cinders. Folders and files. Dockets and statements. The covers of the duty books, with their leather-bound corners, the thick boards of the minute-books and logbooks, the tightly bound spindles of invoices and receipts. The knuckle-bones of rubber stamps. The Captain poked around with the end of a stick and layers of blackened leaves came away from the spines. Inexplicably, in the heart of the fire, new white pages unfolded. They should have torn the covers off the books first and shredded the paper. Stirred up by the stick, a black-edged sheet spiralled up on the smoke and fluttered down next to the Captain's boot. The words were still legible, the handwriting recognisably his own.

The Captain tossed the keys to Voetjie. 'Looks like we're going to need the rest of that wood. And bring the cooler bag, and the grille from the stoep. We'll eat here.'

As soon as they were alone, the Captain began to speak. He told Klopper that his wife had left him. He thought she was having an affair with some Sandton desk jockey, something to do with computers, software. What was he supposed to do now? He was lonely, he was living on takeaways, he had to get a girl in to wash his shirts. His voice thickened and Klopper thought he was going to cry, but he just went on speaking, and he didn't shut up until they saw the headlights coming back down the track.

While Voetjie and Klopper built the bonfire up again, carefully laying the logs on the smouldering papers, the Captain made a smaller fire at the edge of the water. Then they braaied the chops and the wors. When the meat was done the Captain cut the wors into pieces with his pocket knife and speared some of it onto a polystyrene tray for Voetjie, who went to sit on the tail-gate of the bakkie to eat. The other two ate their share straight from the grille.

All this time the bonfire went on burning, with the pages wavering in it like ashen palms, burning and burning.

Sixteen hundred hours, Klopper thought, and wiggled his toes.

'Tell me something, Bate: if these fugu fishes are so poisonous, how come they don't poison themselves? Hey?'

Bate looked at the street. It seemed cold and grey, but that was because the glass was tinted. A scrap of his training floated into his mind: Surveillance. In certain circumstances, you see better out of the corner of your eye. Something to do with the rods and cones. There was some story about listening too . . . you heard better . . . with your mouth open. The cavity of your mouth created a sort of echo chamber. The best attitude to adopt when you thought the enemy was near: turn your face away from him, look at him out of the corner of your eye and keep your mouth open. Bate opened his mouth tentatively. It hurt. He opened wider, and wider, driving the pain from the empty socket up into his ear, into his temple, into the top of his skull. He turned his head slowly until he could see Klopper on the bed from the corner of his eye.

'What the hell are you doing now?'

Once during the meal the wind shifted and blew the smoke over them. It was bittersweet, compounded of leather and ink and sealing wax. For some reason it made Klopper aware of the meat in his mouth, of its texture, the fibres parting between his teeth, the taste of blood on his tongue, but he took a mouthful of beer and swallowed, and it went down. Soon the wind shifted again and carried the smoke out over the water.

'This is the bit I really don't understand. They call it the philosophy of the fugu-eaters . . .'

'Hang on,' said Klopper, 'here he comes.'

'Listen to this: *He who eats fugu fish is stupid . . . but he who does not eat fugu fish is also stupid.* What's that supposed to mean?'

'Beats me.'

Bate went to stand behind the chair and they both looked at the man in the street, a man they knew from photographs, coming towards them in the flesh.

Hair Shirt

In the second autumn of my short life in San Diego, Mel and I flew to Oklahoma City to fetch the car her father had bought for her. The plan was to spend a few days with her parents, getting to know one another, and then drive the car back to the coast.

A road trip was long overdue. In two years of grinding away at pointless jobs, I had hardly been out of the city. When I looked at a map and saw that Route 66 was more or less obligatory, my romance with America, the old flame that had drawn me there, was rekindled. The American landscape was a songbook and its melodies had been playing in my head since I was a child . . . Amarillo, Albuquerque, Memphis Tennessee – they were more evocative than the names of the South African towns I grew up in. It irked me that they had 'By the Time I Get to Phoenix' and we were stuck with 'Sixteen Rietfonteins'.

Mike and Hedda fetched us from the airport and did their best to make me feel at home. They wanted to like me, I could tell, but the obstacles were obvious. I was neither American nor Jewish; I had half a degree and no money. Being an outsider could often be turned to advantage, but it would not work on the Liebmans. For God's sake, Mel said, how many Jews do you think there are in Oklahoma?

I liked them too. Mike was the plain, well-made kind of man the engineering profession attracts, still trim in middle age, and

Hedda was an older version of Mel; she had the same quizzical gaze, the same pale, freckled skin. If anything, the resemblance between them was disconcerting to a young man: I saw exactly what my girlfriend would look like in thirty years' time.

The Liebmans were not especially observant, but they were glad to have their daughter home for Shabbos. The Friday we arrived in Oklahoma City, we had supper together, just the four of us. Hedda said the friends and family could wait, we should have a chance to talk and break the ice. They turned out to be thoughtful, generous people, curious about me and my background but careful not to pry. I had met Americans who were surprised to discover that South Africa was a country, others who were moved to lecture me on the wickedness of apartheid as if the thought had never crossed my mind, and yet others who wanted to swap notes about keeping the blacks in their place, but none of them had been as interested in my point of view as the Liebmans. Although they found apartheid repugnant, they wanted to know more about South Africa, what it felt like, what made it tick. As Jews in a conservative, Christian world, I reasoned, they must understand the complications of belonging. Relieved and disarmed, I was able to express the contradictory feelings about my homeland I usually kept to myself, how I loved it and hated it because, like it or not, the threads of my life had been twisted into its fabric and could not be unravelled.

My situation was more precarious than I let on. I had arrived in California on a tourist visa and overstayed my welcome. You don't have to lie about it, Mel said, they're not going to turn you in to Immigration. But I couldn't tell the truth. When Mike asked about my prospects over dinner, I said I had started out in San Diego only because some of my compatriots found it appealing – it was a lot like Durban, they said – but I had a job waiting for me in San Francisco. Once Mel finished college we might move up there. The two of us had discussed this fantasy, but the details were borrowed from a fellow South African, a university acquaintance with a degree and a career in computers.

The conversation soon strayed from my imaginary future, sparing me the discomfort of having to elaborate the lie. The evening passed pleasantly and I seemed to make a good impression. When the meal was over, Mike carried the coffee tray through to the living room and switched on the TV for the sports results. 'Go and smoke a cigar with Dad,' Mel said, giving me a quick kiss and taking the gravy boat out of my hands. 'Do the stuff the men are supposed to do.'

As I was leaving the room, I noticed the candles in silver sticks on the dresser. I blew one of them out and was bending to blow out the second when Mel grabbed my arm. 'What are you doing? They're supposed to burn down on their own!' She scrabbled in the drawer of the dresser for matches. We could hear her mother loading the dishwasher in the next room. I fumbled for my lighter and relit the candle, while Mel waved a napkin to shoo away the fumes of the wick. 'Idiot!' She was smiling but there was an edge of annoyance in her voice.

'How was I to know?'

We laughed about it afterwards. Stop fretting, she said, it's not as if you threw a brick through the window of the shul!

But the blunder unnerved me. It made me realise how anxious she was that I fit in. We had fun that weekend, visiting her old haunts and looking up old friends, and I got on with her parents, talking books with Hedda and suspension bridges with Mike. But in their home I kept thinking: are the curtains meant to be open in the middle of the night? Does that thimble of salt have some ritual purpose unknown to me? Am I allowed to use this cup?

On the Monday, Mel decided we should make a trip to see her Uncle Colley. Supposedly, we were giving the Honda a test run before we braved the long drive home, but there was more to it than that.

. . .

We stayed overnight in a motel off the I-40 just across the Arkansas state line and drove up into the mountains the next morning. We had missed the full blaze of the fall colours, but the muted reds and yellows of the trees had a smouldering beauty of their own. As soon as we left the interstate, we seemed to have gone off at a tangent from the modern world. We passed tumbledown shacks with screen doors closed on their dim interiors and smoke creeping from their chimneys. The further we went, the more primitive they looked. Don't expect neon lights and running water at Colley's, I'd been warned, it ain't the Best Western. Still, I had no idea that people lived like this in Ronald Reagan's America. It might have been some remote corner of the Transkei. The deer-hunting season had started and the woods were full of hunters. Flickers of gunmetal through the trees, a glimpse of a crouched figure in a bright jerkin stalking through a clearing, the occasional shot thumping down off the heights convinced me that we were driving back into another century.

Colley lived alone. He was – I hesitate to use the term – the black sheep of the family and they were embarrassed by him and proud of him at the same time. He was no close kin of the Liebmans: one of Hedda's aunts had married some cousin or half-brother of his. The fact that he was not a blood relation, and did not have to be accounted for in their genes, made it possible to claim him for the family history as a living link to what was rough-hewn and untamed in the American spirit.

I was under strict instructions not to use the word 'hillbilly' in Arkansas. But that was only part of Colley's ambiguous charm. The other part – the main part – was his hair. He had too much of it. I don't mean he had more hair on his head than the average man: his entire body (so I'd been told) was covered with it. The condition was so severe that as a young man he'd joined a freak show and been displayed at state fairs as the wolfman – dogman – apeman – depending on the preferences of the day.

Mel had told me Colley's story long ago. Everyone who found out we were going to see him had given it another twist. I wasn't sure what to believe. When his name came up, people swapped glances or suppressed a laugh. Sometimes the whole thing felt like the kind of prank you play on foreigners to show how gullible they are. For all I knew, I was being initiated into the family through a test of my humour or forbearance.

The road had dwindled to a track and I was starting to wonder how much more we could expect of the car when we finally reached Colley's ramshackle cabin. As we drew up on the bare patch of ground that passed for a front yard, he rose from a rocking chair and came to the edge of the porch.

At first glance he seemed disappointingly ordinary, not even bearded, a big man in washed-out dungarees and a checked shirt. His face had something raw about it, like a vegetable that has been blanched and hastily peeled, and his long, pale hands hung down at his sides, tapering towards the earth like taproots. A joke at my expense, I thought. Or has his condition – I didn't know what to call it – abated over the years? But when he greeted me, and my fingertips pressed against the soft, greasy back of his hand, it occurred to me that the skin had been shaved.

He gave Mel a hug. Then he pulled his hat over his brow and helped me fetch the bags from the car. He wanted to carry them into the cabin, but she insisted we'd sleep in the RV as usual. After a tussle of wills, we all went round to the back where an old motorhome stood on blocks. It was damp and mushroomy inside. The bare mattress looked like a block of old cheddar.

Colley wanted to show us off. He led me out front, pointed to one of the rockers and took the other. There was coffee left over from breakfast on the stove, and Mel poured us each a cup and brought out a chair. We spent the rest of the morning on the porch, where the hunters passing in their pickups could note that he had company.

Everyone stopped to talk. They wanted to know about the deer, about who had got lucky yesterday and where, but mainly they were curious about the visitors. Once their memories had been jogged, a few of them recognised Mel, who'd been coming here since she was a little girl.

Colley's neck of the woods was not on the tourist route and he was particularly proud of me. 'This boy here's from Africky,' he said more than once. 'He's from plumb across the pond.' It wasn't long before I disappointed him.

A man called Mason and his son, who farmed together on the other side of the valley, came along in a pickup and Colley decided I should join their hunting party. He insisted; he even went to fetch a rifle. I would have gone too – being shown off like a curiosity was making me irritable – but while he was inside Mel leant over and said in my ear, 'Don't leave me alone with him.'

'Why not?'

'It's just not a good idea.'

'What should I say? I don't want to offend him.'

'Make some excuse. Say you've got an eye problem or something.'

Colley came back with the rifle in the crook of his arm.

'I know nothing about rifles,' I said. 'I've never fired one before.'

This was a lie. I'd been in the army and learnt to use everything from a popgun to a Browning, and I'd gone hunting too, although I hadn't pulled the trigger myself.

The Masons looked aghast. Never used a gun? And he says he comes from Africky.

'The boys'll show you how,' Uncle Colley said.

'I don't believe in hunting, actually. I mean, I don't mind if other people do it, but I'd rather not join in.'

He exchanged a knowing glance with his neighbour. For a moment, I was annoyed with Mel for making me play the city-boy, but my thoughts quickly turned to her reasons. Was she scared of him? And, if so, why had we come?

The Masons went off along the track. We sat in the rockers. There was nothing else to do.

In the course of the morning, I had a good look at Colley. Not that there was much to be seen: he kept the shirt buttoned to his throat and wore boots under the dungarees. His hair was cropped into a blunt block on top of his head. It was strange, I thought, that a man who apparently had too much hair should look like he was wearing a wig.

Around noon, he sent me into the yard behind the cabin to stack firewood. Grateful for the distraction, I put my back into it, working the tension and tedium out of my muscles. When I came back, Mel was balanced on his knee, with his long fingers clasping her hips and the heel of his boot drumming. Playing horsey, you could say. She rolled her eyes at me as she squirmed off his lap. Over her shoulder, he was smirking as if I was the biggest fool he'd ever met.

It was lunchtime. We followed him along a path through the trees to a lot where a dozen pickups were parked, one model after another like a row of old journals, and we climbed into the newest one and drove back down the road we had come on. He doesn't need to work, Mike had told me, he owns shares in an oilfield in Oklahoma and he's got more money than he knows what to do with.

At a rest stop on the interstate, we had chicken baskets and fries and big glasses of iced tea. Halfway through the meal, I noticed the five o'clock shadow on the backs of his hands.

We returned to the cabin. Still there was nothing to do and we sat on the porch again. As the afternoon wore on, the hunters started coming down out of the hills with the deer they'd shot. Mason and his son had a doe draped over the hood. 'This one's yours,' Mason said to me. 'She's got your name on her.' The kill looked underweight to me – there were rules about the size of the animals you could take – but, as a man who knew nothing about hunting, I thought I should hold my tongue.

Uncle Colley had the boy carry it around to the smokehouse. There was some spring left in the lithe body, and when he slung it across his shoulders it twisted in his grip as if it were trying to get away.

Alone that night, clinging together on the crumbling sponge like survivors of some natural disaster, Mel and I whispered and giggled for an hour.

'What an old goat,' I said, 'he can't keep his paws off you. You should have warned me.'

'He's harmless.'

'Really? You seem quite scared of him.'

'I know how to deal with him. I just don't want to make it harder than it should be.'

'Isn't it weird, though, the way he keeps touching you? I mean, you could make him stop.'

'It's not that simple.'

'What do you mean?'

'You have to imagine that he's been alone all his life. I'm sure he's never had a normal relationship. He's starved for affection. Doesn't it make you sad?'

I woke the next morning to the sound of running water. For a drowsy moment I thought I was in my own bed and Mel was taking a shower. Just as I realised where I was, the splashing stopped and I heard a low moan, and then silence. Pulling the blanket around my shoulders against the early-morning chill, I knelt on the mattress and looked through the blinds.

In the clearing behind the cabin, Colley was sitting in a metal tub with his head between his knees, enveloped in a fuzzy cocoon of steam. Mel was bent over him, lathering his back with a block of soap. Her skin was pale in the morning light and soft as tissue paper, so clear and thin I could see the angles of her hipbones and shoulder blades. I cannot say I doubted for an instant that the creature in the tub was Colley. What else could it be? And yet two certainties condensed in my mind at the same time like images superimposed on one another: it was Uncle Colley and something else, an animal covered in thick brown fur that had followed the smell of fresh blood out of the woods and let itself be domesticated.

Mel put the soap down on an upturned bucket and reached for a long-handled brush. The shaggy hound moaned in anticipation. With the ease of a circus girl who did this every morning, she scrubbed at his back, working the foam into his fur, shoving it all one way and then raking it the other. He submitted to this painful pleasure, drawing his head down between his shoulders against the thrust of the bristles and then stretching out his neck again as the brush went down his spine.

He looked to me like the dog-headed men in a medieval bestiary or one of those monsters out of Africa with eyes in its chest or the head of a lion. Except that it was the other way round: the head of a man on the body of a beast. I have always been more susceptible to myth than psychology. Perhaps that's why this vision did not repulse me.

She poked him with the handle of the brush and he stood up. In an instant, the book learning was sluiced away and he was simply a man, a big man with too much hair on his body, two naked hands and a naked prick, and a big round head with a patch of fur on its crown.

There was a hose attached to the rainwater tank and Mel opened the tap and held her thumb over the end. He yelled and capered in the jet, feeble though it was, splashing suds over the sides of the tub, and the water ran off him, driving channels through the hair down his thighs, while the cloak of steam blew away in tatters. As a young man I was prone to jealousy, yet I felt nothing but a shiver of recognition.

I lay down and pulled the stinking blanket over my head. If I went outside, I knew, everything would change, the story would have a different ending, but I had no idea whether it would be better or worse. What would I say?

In the event, I did not have to make a decision because the door opened and shut. I pretended to be sleeping. Mel slipped in beside me. When I turned over and clasped her shivering, soap-scented body, the small of her back felt strange to my touch, cold and damp and covered with goosebumps.

Later that morning, as we were preparing to leave, Colley brought a ladder into the cabin and sent me up it to fetch a cardboard box from the musty cave in the rafters. There was something he wanted to give me as a going-away present. It was a red flannel shirt. God knows how long it had been up there. The thing was filthy; it smelt of bacon grease and sweat, but he insisted that I try it on. Ants, or some other insect I could not imagine, had been nesting in one of the sleeves and when I pushed my arm through it a lump of hard red earth fell out of the cuff.

He wouldn't let me take it off. He told me it fitted perfectly, although the cuffs hung down past my fingertips, and he winked at Mel so theatrically that I couldn't fail to notice.

I was still wearing the hunting shirt when we drove away. As soon as we rounded the first bend in the road, I stopped the car, pulled the thing over my head and flung it into the undergrowth.

The day after we got back from Arkansas, the aunts and uncles and family friends came to celebrate Shabbos at the Liebmans. In the afternoon, I helped Mike put the leaf in the dining-room table and bring the extra chairs up from the basement.

Mike's brother Morris was the last to arrive. He was a psychologist, although he looked like a businessman in his dove-grey suit and burnished wingtips. His bow tie, a rash of pink polka dots on creamy silk, was a whimsical flourish with an ambiguous message. 'Relax,' it said, 'I don't take myself as seriously as you do.' But I heard, 'Beware! Don't think I'm harmless because I'm wearing this silly tie.'

He hunted me down in the living room, where the men were chatting while the women put the finishing touches to the dinner, and pulled a chair up so that we could talk.

'I've never actually met someone from Darkest Africa,' he said, 'let alone a representative of the master race.' And then he laid a puffy hand over my own to show that he was joking. When I spoke, he tilted his head to one side, profoundly attentive.

He started out by telling me that he despised apartheid. He imagined that no one could live in South Africa without going mad. It would make you sick, he expected. He imagined and expected many things. 'I imagine it makes you feel awful,' he said. 'I expect it keeps you awake at night.' Within a minute I felt like fleeing, but the arm of his chair was pressed into the padded side of the sofa like a bony elbow in my ribs. Only joking, he said, and gave me another jab. I was relieved when we were called to the table, disappointed to find him directly opposite, appraising me over the rim of his wine glass as if he could see through me.

'Our visitor from Africa should say the blessing,' he said when we were all gathered around the table.

I declined. He insisted, until I had to say: 'I'm not Jewish.' The yarmulke I had pinned to the back of my head suddenly felt like a ridiculous disguise.

'Forgive me,' Uncle Morris said, 'I just assumed.'

Mike said the broche, and as soon as we were seated the awkwardness was submerged in talk and laughter. Mel gave my leg a reassuring squeeze under the table.

It was a country meal with Yiddish trimmings. There was no chicken soup, although one of the aunts had brought chopped liver, which was served with crackers rather than kichel. The main course was quail. Hedda warned us: 'Watch your teeth.'

We spoke about Uncle Colley, of course. Morris imagined how surprised I must have been to find a man living in such a primitive state. The way he said 'primitive' was insinuating, as if he was quoting a word I had used myself, one which passed a judgement that rebounded on me. He had a way of looking at me that suggested he knew me better than anyone else at the table. 'Living up there in the woods,' he said, 'you need a strong stomach to keep the man's company.'

The picture of Colley and Mel came into my mind, and along with it a shameful sense of betrayal. Unsure what I had seen passing between them, half-convinced I had dreamt it all, I had not said a word, and neither had she.

There was no sign of birdshot in my quail, although everyone else was fishing bits of black lead from their mouths. Halfway through the meal though, I began to feel strange. My skin crawled. I should have said something at once, but I didn't want to cause a fuss.

The conversation turned to medicine. Perhaps it started with the question of whether anything might have been done for Colley, or perhaps one of the old people was simply discussing their aches and pains. Uncle Morris bemoaned the wasteful excesses of modern healers, the cascades of pills and potions, the bloody surgeries. Doctors were always reaching for the scalpel. He mentioned Chris Barnard, who had put the heart of a black man – or was it a baboon? – in an ailing white body, in the body – pulling a face at me – of a Jew. Everyone laughed. He did a toothy impression of Barnard that seemed to me a parody of my own accent. He began to speak about eczema. When Mel and I discussed it afterwards, after I'd recovered, she insisted this part of the conversation came later, when Morris was trying to make a diagnosis, *saving my life*, I was disorientated, but in my memory it comes before, he is suggesting the diseases of the skin to which I might fall prey, predicting them if you like, urticaria, prurigo, suppurating boils. They were all possible, indeed likely, they were to be imagined and expected. While he was busy with the list, I opened a gap between two buttons of my shirt and saw that my belly was covered with red spots. My skin was burning. I put my hand under my shirt and scratched and peered again through the gap. It looked like chickenpox. The rash was already rising on my neck. I should have said something, but I carried on eating and listening to the talk around me, following a line here and a phrase there, catching hold of none of it, letting the meanings sink beneath their accents. Then Hedda's sister was bringing in the strawberry fool and Hedda was waving at me from across the table as if we were on opposite sides of a river in spate. The welts had appeared on my cheeks apparently and my neck was puffing out like a bullfrog's.

Morris took charge. He gave instructions for an ambulance to be called. Then he scratched through the medicine cabinet and crushed a couple of tablets into a glass of water and got the mixture down my throat before it closed up entirely. They put me on the sofa while they waited for help to come. I was gasping for breath. Mel held my hand and cried. Her mother's drawn face came and went over her shoulder, echoing out of a distant future in which an old man on his deathbed, surrounded by a little circle of family and friends, turned out to be me.

A numb sense of calm seeped into my limbs – Morris had added a tranquilliser to the mix, reasoning astutely that what needed managing most was my anxiety – and I heard voices and spoons chiming on teacups. Morris especially: 'You never know what will come to the surface,' he said. 'The skin never lies.'

. . .

We drove back to San Diego a few days later than planned. I recuperated in the guest room, laid out on the sleeper couch like a corpse, with the blinds drawn against the light. Hedda joked once too often about the judgement I had passed on her cooking.

The kicks I got on Route 66 were less intoxicating than I'd anticipated, more in keeping with a Honda hatchback than a Ford Thunderbird. My illness had made us late and we had jobs to get back to, so we stayed on the interstate most of the way, but once or twice we went off to follow the old highway. I drove and Mel read the maps. From time to time, she also read aloud from the novels by Steinbeck and Kafka which Hedda had packed for us like a picnic, the passages she had marked with playing cards about the great mother road that took the Joads west to California, the way we were going now, and the railway line that brought Karl Rossmann over mountain passes and bridges to work in the great Theatre of Oklahoma, where everyone was welcome.

On the way out of Oklahoma City, we passed a sign that said, 'Caution! Hitch-hikers may be escaping convicts.' Just a mile further on, as if to prove that the state authorities had a point, we came to a man hitch-hiking. Picturing the prison garb under his business suit, we laughed and laughed. It kept us laughing all the way to the coast.

Winter was settling over Oklahoma, turning it pale and brittle. The countryside reminded me of the Free State, the stubble fields and silvery grass, the vast empire of the sky that made your head float off your shoulders, the grain silos in farming towns where the railway lines still defined a right and a wrong side of the tracks, the little divided Western towns that were so much like platteland dorps and their townships. A complicated homesickness began to dismantle the makeshift version of myself I had constructed in California. I thought of sharing this feeling with Mel, but she had never seen the Free State, and I knew in the backwoods of my body that she never would.

101 Detectives

He knew there were tricks – no – not tricks, techniques, there are techniques for getting to see what you're not supposed to. Let's say the register at reception in the hotel lobby. You drop the pen or you fake a cough and ask for a glass of water, and while the clerk is distracted you quickly turn the book your way and scan the page for what you're after. Let's say the room number of a particular person. Or let's say the name of a particular person occupying a certain room the number of which is no mystery. He knew all that.

But as it happened, the counter was a slab of granite and there was no book to mar its smooth extension, not even a computer screen, which complicated things. Also there was nothing he needed to know. For now. He was simply waiting for the receptionist to give him his key and number so that he could go up to his room. This lack of knowing, or rather this lack of a need to know, made him feel less like a Detective. And the feeling rankled because he was unsure what kind of Detective he really was to begin with.

While he was examining this lack, trying to locate it precisely in his body, the receptionist handed him his key. She pointed out the Breakfast Room to the left and mentioned the hours. Then she pointed out the Assembly Room through an archway to the right, and beyond that the lift. She also offered to call a porter but he said no, he could manage, he was travelling light, just the one suitcase with wheels. He was the kind of Detective who did not like to be followed to his room. That was one thing he was sure of.

When he passed the Assembly Room on his way to the lift he saw a noticeboard on an easel, an oblong of black plastic to which white plastic letters could be attached. Welcome! the board said. 101 Detectives: Sub-Saharan Africa. Meet and Greet 6 p.m. Private (eye) function :). He glanced at his watch and saw that it was 3 p.m. and this pleased him, because it gave him enough time to settle in and take a shower and maybe nap and then think for a while about what kind of Detective he was or wanted to be.

His room was on the third floor, the top floor, and he had booked it for that reason. For the escape routes. But he got out on the second floor in case anyone was watching the dial in the lobby that ticked off the numbers. Then he walked swiftly up one flight to the third and went along the corridor to his room, pulling the suitcase on wheels, noting cupboard doors and emergency exits and the herringbone pattern in the carpet and especially the trolley full of mops and brooms and crumpled sheets that might spell trouble.

The key was a plastic card with holes in it. When he inserted it into the lock a green light blinked and then he stood to one side and pushed the door open. He wanted to case the joint, but the door was on a spring-loaded elbow and shut itself. So he reinserted the card in the lock and wedged the door open with his foot. Voices. For a moment he froze. But then he saw from the flickering light in the room that it was just the TV set talking to itself. He went in.

The voice was describing the facilities and attractions but the image on the screen was still. A lion licking its paw like a kitten. He remembered this later. There was a message on the screen: Sunny Bonani welcomes Mr Joseph Blumenfeld to 101 Detectives:

Sub-Saharan Africa. We are at your service. The message was in white letters but 'Joseph Blumenfeld' was in red and it leapt out at him like a suspect from the shadows. For a moment he froze and a tight fist of fear clenched in his gut. That name rang a bell.

And then he remembered that he was undercover. I am Joseph Blumenfeld, he thought. For a moment he felt like an impostor. Until he recalled the words of his mentor, Long John de Lange, who used to say that all Detectives sometimes feel like charlatans, it comes with the territory, and the memory of his dear friend and teacher, with his quirky fluency in dead languages and his flawed understanding of the martial arts, cheered him. He found the remote and switched off the TV. Then he sat on the bed and looked around.

Nothing exceptional. Yet he felt at home. He felt at home in this unremarkable room, which he had entered a moment ago. And that made him wonder whether he was not at heart a very ordinary Detective. He had worked so hard to identify his flaws and quirks, those traits that would set him apart from his flawed and quirky peers. But now he wondered whether being unremarkable might not be his special quality. Although he suspected that many another Detective was ordinary too. Exceptional, ordinary, it was a matter of choice. Hobson's.

Hobson would be a good name when travelling incognito, he thought, reaching into his jacket pocket for notebook and pen. His fingers brushed an edge there and he froze for a moment. Then he recalled the wide-eyed man at the airport who had pressed a leaflet into his hand and how he had folded it in half lengthways without even looking at it and put it away in his pocket. He wondered whether that had been wise. He took out the paper and unfolded it. The cold fist in his gut unclenched.

How toxic are you? he read. Take this simple test and find out. There was a list of questions with two small blocks before each one for Yes or No. □□1. Have you felt fatigued for no apparent reason? □□2. Do you sometimes feel 'wooden' and lifeless? □□3. Do you feel less alert than you used to? □□4. Do you sometimes get a feeling of light-headedness? In his head, which felt light and wooden simultaneously, like a balsawood lantern on his flesh-and-bone shoulders, he ticked one Yes block after the other.

Yes. He felt less alert than he used to. As he tried to locate this feeling in his body, Louella Scarlozzi, the femme fatale of the Coroner's Office, Italian-American, gruff, tall, came to mind. He flew in through her ear, down an earhole where wax clung like wasps' nests, past the hammer and anvil, making a beeline for her secret thoughts. What kind of Detective am I? Eardrum or tympanum? Gullet or oesophagus? Pussy or pudenda? A Detective needs a language almost as much as a language needs a Detective.

He turned over the leaflet. More pertinent questions. (De Lange: Never mind the answers. Ask the right questions.) □□5. Do you feel irritable without reason or cause? □□6. Do you have less energy and vitality than you used to? □□7. Do you find it difficult to get excited about people or things? Yes, yes, yes. These affirmations fell on him like blows and he slumped down on the duvet. □□8. Do you have trouble reading or learning new things? Yes. □□9. Do you feel anxious and don't know why?

The ceiling was greasy and pockmarked. It looked like acned skin. But what caused the fist to clench in his gut was that it seemed so low. Vigilance! He sprang up and gazed about. Neglecting the basics. Am I that kind of Detective? He paced out the distance from door to window. There was a ballpoint pen on the dresser with Sunny Bonani printed on its barrel. He used this pen to write the figure on the bottom of the leaflet next to the name L. Ron Hubbard.

L for what? It was suspicious. The whole name was the undercover sort of thing Long John de Lange would make up. L for Leather. Were there Scientological Detectives? He had never before considered the question of religion in his capacity as a

Detective. A failure on his part. One of the first things a Detective ought to get clear in his mind. He thought about the preponderance of obsessive-compulsive Jews and guilt-ridden Catholics inhabiting Detective World. Also Presbyterians and Buddhists. Who faced the facts with equanimity.

He himself was a lapsed Methodist. He wondered if Methodism made for meticulous investigation and if there were any Methodist Detectives of note. He would have to consider the literature. These thoughts about research and religion pulled him in two different directions. An unbearable pressure began to build up in his chest or his gut, he couldn't be sure, as if two cold fists were clenching and unclenching, pumping tension into his abdomen. To defuse the situation, he opened the minibar. For a moment he froze.

As he gazed at the little bottles of Gilbey's and J&B, his mind went back to 101 Detectives: South Pacific and the amount of drinking it had demanded. Drinking and Detection go together like Gin and Tonic, Smith and Wesson, Assault and Battery. He remembered the dry Detectives clutching bottles of mineralwasser in the Kontiki Lounge while their sodden colleagues languished under beach umbrellas outside, nursing their fatal flaws in big careworn hands, listening to the icy chiming of the quirks in their shot glasses.

Fridge-light fell on the scuffed toes of his shoes. He remembered this later. What would his sharp-eyed counterparts say? *Falling apart.* He wondered why he hadn't buffed the black brogues with the lanolin-impregnated sponge that was resting on a shelf in the wardrobe. In all likelihood. Why he hadn't opened the doors and drawers, looking for things disturbingly ordinary. Haunting in their ordinariness. A loose thread in the trouser press, a dead bulb in the reading lamp. A careless Detective is a dead Detective.

He took the room-service menu from the dresser and sat again on the bed. On the cover of the menu was a lion licking its paw. He had seen that somewhere before. He opened the menu and looked at the prices. Exorbitant. He was a poor Detective, that was one thing he was sure of. A down-at-heel gumshoe. He was not travelling on an expense account, did not fly business class, did not have pals who could lay on the Johnnie Walker Blue.

Penniless. He put the menu aside and began to open the doors of the wardrobe until he found the one with the mirror. He looked at his mouth as he said: *Penurious. Impecunious. Parsimonious.* In what damp recess of my mind have these words incubated? He turned his head one way and another. The brow: high this way, middle that. The mouth: small and pinched, broad and smiling. There are two sides to every story, coin, playing card, seven-single, football match, tango.

Detectives at leisure. Tanned Americans with their pockets full of beachsand, pale Swedes tramping snow up the stairs, Australians fragrant with sunblock SPF 30+. De Lange: Never trust a Detective with his own motorboat. True. But there is more to life than Detection. Even the poorest practitioner needs to get his mind off the job. He considered the hobbies: poker, polo, needlepoint, marathon running, chess, snorkelling, traditional Irish fiddle music, angling, philately, taxidermy, radio-controlled model aircraft, the cult of the budgerigar.

It surfaced in his mind like a bubble from a severed air line. 101 Detectives: Cancún. The pointless rigmarole of introduction – *Hello, my name is Carlos and I'm a Detective* – when every one of them was undercover. That clown Tobias from Frankfurt had swallowed a contact lens on the plane and was edgy. And then Aliber who was running the show brought in the sniffer dog, an overexcitable German shepherd, for some party game or other and Tobias went ballistic.

Odd how the drinkers always banded together. When everyone else had gone to bed, the Protestants would be trying to drink the Catholics under the table. In Detective World, as in any other, like sought like. The costive sleuths of Scandinavian extraction and logical bent (Gustaf Magnusson, Magnus Andersson, Anders Gustafsson) smuggled their home-baked rye and fermented fish into the breakfast room. Even the Lutheran haemophiliac had company, an agnostic bleeder from Skipton who had met the Yorkshire Ripper.

Why did he keep coming to these things? He always went away saying: Never again. And then a new summons came, in serial-killer typography, on the back of a handbill for homeopathic remedies, pinned under the wiper blade of the Ford Bantam in the dead of night, in mirror script, in red lipstick on the bathroom cabinet, in schoolgirl Mandarin, on a yellow Post-it stuck to a brick, lobbed through a window. The marketing people never gave up.

And neither should he. Perhaps it was the friendship that kept him coming back, the fellowship, the camaraderie. Only a Detective knew what another Detective went through. Only another Detective understood what went into casing the joint, tracing the movement, combing the printout, testing the hypothesis, cracking the code, wearing the wire, calling for backup, taking the fall, cleaning the wound, typing the report, citing the reference. No explanations were needed, just a cast in the eye.

He had his connections, his 101 crew. At every Meet and Greet there were one or two nearly familiar characters. Chums. He would scour their craggy features for clues while they punched his shoulder or smell their receding hairlines when they leant in close for a battering embrace. What was that oceanic note? Norwegian salmon? Guatemalan devilfish? Herring. It brought back 101 Detectives: Den Haag. Better say nothing. Taciturn was also a style. Perhaps even his.

He should analyse these over-friendly colleagues. A common denominator might help him find his place in Detective World.

A pattern. He conjured up a face, Chief Inspector Connell of the Gorbals, but all that came back was the mutton-chop whiskers. And then, unbidden, the loose-limbed frame of Dr Louella Scarlozzi, followed by the ethanol undertone of her handcream. Once, when she'd opened her handbag to look for her shades, a rubber glove had fallen out.

Suddenly he missed his wife. He was a married Detective. That was one thing he was sure of. One whose wife and kids had paid the price for his work. Whose wife had stuck by him through thick and thin. Mostly thin. The world was full of angry divorced Detectives, whose wives kept the kids away from them, and bitter bachelor Detectives who spent their nights in bars. He was not one of those.

He missed his kids. Little Davy who wanted to be a Detective like his dad. Little Sookie the jolly little June bug who was having trouble learning to read. Little Okefenokee who could play Wagner on the pennywhistle. Not-so-little Lilo who could count to leventy-leven on her thumbs. Lovable little scallywags. He should take them all something. Something better than a last-minute box of Smarties from the Duty Free on his way home.

He shut the wardrobe and opened the minibar. The Toblerone was exorbitant and calorific, but no one was counting. He pushed the bar out of the cardboard wrapper with his forefinger, peeled away the silver foil, snapped off three blocks and put them in his mouth. They were cold. He pressed them against his palate with his tongue. Swiss design. Very odd, he thought. Like eating the spine of a chocolate mammal.

A bittersweet prospect: Joseph Blumenfeld, Morbidly Obese Detective. Confined to bed in his spongebobbed room, conducting his business from a wireless bellytop nested in the flab, sausage fingers flying. Cut off from the hurly-burly and therefore even better suited to being a Detective. Strange to say. He pushed another five vertebrae into his mouth. He could pile on the pounds. There was still time, if he put his mouth to it.

Many things had been sent to try a Detective over the years: opium addiction, alcoholism, blindness, Catholicism, melancholia, loss of limb, obsessive compulsion, motion sickness, hydrophobia, lycanthropy, lack of stature, tone deafness. No burden was so great it could not be turned to account. Who was he to complain about a mild case of panic disorder, high cholesterol levels and subcutaneous acne? No one's feet are exactly the same size.

The world was his oyster. And yet there were many kinds of Detective he would never be. He would never be a terribly black Detective, no matter how hard he practised. He would not even be a convincing African Detective. Not that the idea appealed much. People asked too many questions, there were too many forms to complete. Better to be a Detective of the World. Of Detective World.

Chances of being a lady Detective were nearly zero. No ma'am, he would never be such. Disadvantaged Detective? Zero. Persecuted Detective? Less than. He would not flee atrocities or overcome obstacles. Not really. He would never be a lesbian Muslim Detective of Turkish origins. Not in a month of Sundays. Resident in Kreuzberg. No ways. With one eye. Fuck that. Mother with Alzheimer's. What's the matter with you?

It was sad. But lodged in that sad, like a slug in a gut, was a lump of joy. A wingnut in a sausage roll? There was comfort in the narrowing of possibility and there was freedom in restraint. He would never be a retired prize-winning jockey Detective, bones were too big. But it was not too late for riding lessons, if he could overcome his hippophobia.

Shit, shave and shampoo, as they say in the service. Let's do it! Chop chop. Before he stepped into the cubicle, he hung his linen jacket on the towel rail. When – if – he hit the Meet and Greet later, he would be professionally crumpled or not at all. De Lange: Never trust a Detective with creases in his pants and none in his jacket. Damn straight.

He shouldered the door and thumbed the lug until the jet was scalding. He felt his lethargy burning off, sluiced away over belly and thigh, going down the tubes with suds and musk-scented conditioner from the little lab specimen bottles. He flew down the pipe where sludge and sewerage and scum were caulked like hives. He let go laziness, fancy, illusion. All ears. Totally nose.

Then he palmed off the spume and grubbed the flange until the jet grew icy. He mugged up to the stream. His nerves jangled through. Now he manned up and hunkered down and so forth. Drying off, double time, vigilance rose to the skin. Dress for the occasion, it says on the label. Costume is crucial and so are prepositions. He remembered this later.

There was a towelling dressing gown on a hook in the wardrobe and he put it on. An embroidered crest over the heart showed a lion rampant, licking its paw. It came back to him now. Towelling slippers too. He snuggled his feet into them and wriggled his toes. Comfy. Verbs ending in -uggle and -iggle. He thought about that. Nothing escaped him.

Plan for the worst-case scenario, as it says in the manual. In every cockamamie manual between here and Timbuctoo or maybe Poughkeepsie. Somewhere else's somewhere else. His language was acting up and it scared him. No argument. Cellophane? He hooked it out from under the bed with a wire coathanger: the slim plastic wrapper from an individually wrapped toothpick. He bagged it.

Then he went to the window, kinked one blade of the venetian blind with his forefinger, and brought his eye close. The parking lot was a sticky plate of black gumbo and yellow herringbones. There was just one car down there in a viscous smear of sunlight, a late model Subaru with snowchains on the tyres. A small herd of zebra.

For a moment he thought it was the hire-car he had driven in from the airport. But that was 101 Detectives: Yellow River. They run into one another if you fail to keep the edges straight. Now he remembered the bus ride, men with machetes slashing the fenders, rocks bouncing off the hood. Burning tyres. *Sub-Saharan Africa, man!* Bang bang.

He stood there for a long time, looking down on the lot, until the tip of his finger grew numb. The windows of the car were misted over, he thought, as if someone was in there breathing. The sun dropped. The shadow of the lodge seeped out towards the Subaru like a pool of blood from a gut-shot motherfucker.

He looked for words. For a precise phrase to make something happen. *Here he comes now.* No. *Here come trouble.* Who the hell speaks like that? *What have we here.* No, it was all wrong. *Fuck me George.* Better. *Sonofabitch.* One word. That's the ticket, trick, technique. Few words as possible. *Fuck. Hey. Yo.* But no one came.

He kicked off the slippers. He was feeling more precise again, calibrated, indexed. He paced out the distance from door to window, heel to toe, and wrote the number on the leaflet. The question snagged his eye again: How toxic are you? He should have followed his father's advice and become a pharmacist. Or a quantity surveyor.

Then again he would bet a pound to a pinch of table salt that every second quantity surveyor wished he was a Detective. People thought Detective World was glamorous, they thought it was all cocktails and cadavers. They had no idea how hard it was. All the quirks had been taken. That was half the problem.

Say he learnt to play the ukulele. He could be the music-making, mountain-climbing Detective. Then one fine day, as he toiled up to base camp, it would come on the breeze: Follow every rainbow . . . Yep, that broad with the banjo, who was climbing the third-highest peak on every continent, had beaten him to it.

Then again he loved card tricks and newsprint and foreign tongues. He could fold newsbills into pigeons, he could pull pidgins out of a hat. What would take you further in Detective World? he wondered. Mumbo-jumbo or hocus-pocus? Mumbo-pocus! Be paper-foldy, magic-makey Detective. Jolly-fine day, come by base camp, who dat? Kumbaya my Lord.

He thought about Polkinghorn, the Detective's Detective, who had the earbud franchise. The Polkster, the Hornster, the Budster. Many affectionate nicknames ending with -ster. He was 101-Detectives-in-one. When he fell off the paddywagon and broke his panama there wasn't a dry eye in Detective World. *All buds to every body.* And vice versa.

Loved a corpse outlined in chalk on the living-room floor. Every home should have one, a dead thing, a visual effect, a body of evidence. If only there were enough of them to supply the demand. There were never enough victims to go round. The Polksters were arm-wrestling the Hornsters for cadavers.

Four thirty already! The second hand swept past with its fist clenched. He thought too much and did too little. A Detective had to strike a balance between thought and action or be carried off in mid-deduction before his work was done. All the great Detectives were dead before their time.

All the great Detectives are dead full stop. Or so it seemed to him. He called them to mind, the gentlemen with meerschaum pipes and watchchains, in their trenchcoats and fedoras, their chequered vests and pasts. Flaws were grander back then, but more forgivable; quirks were truer and more endearing.

The moderns had no manners, no sense of decorum or shame. They were far too concerned with wounds. Their minds were narrow and their mouths were foul. Motherfucker this and cocksucker that. Their flaws were pathologies, their quirks were disorders. You could hardly tell the Detectives from the non-.

Everybody is a Detective now, everybody and his brother. That's the other half of the problem, he thought. Wherever you go, you trip over a Detective, peering under a bed or crouched behind a bush, bristling with equipment, probing and prodding, and dabbing to see if it glows.

They're over-equipped, under-trained and ill-mannered. Case in point: Detective Spivis of 101 Detectives: Baden-Württemberg with his Iron Maiden T-shirt and his thick-lipped trainers. Tossing peanuts into his mouth from an unsalted stash in a moonbag. Talking in monosyllables at the Meet and Greet. One of the boys.

To think that this slob with a ring through his eyebrow is top dog of Detective World. He has a loft in the city and a cabin in the woods, but he winters in the South of France. Changes his address more often than his socks.

Then the sayings of De Lange chided him. This one in particular: Detection is its own reward. The maestro was right, he thought, envy is unseemly in a Detective. So what if there are too many files on your desk. It comes with the territory.

He should get on with it. He had earbuds, he had tweezers, he had a little torch. He had a dozen bottles with childproof lids. He should swab something and see if it changed colour. Stub the lug, rootle it down in the grab-bag.

He dug this snub-nosed lingo slubbing out of his pug-ugly mug. It was good. It was endings in -ub and -ug. He could get a grip on stuff with it. Solve shit. Make some moves he needed to get down in Detective World.

Always be first at the scene of the accident, quick through the barricades, flashing your face like a badge. Always be first at the buffet, nosing the canapés, tossing them back by the fistful. Never be first at the Meet and Greet.

Meeting and greeting. His heart sank at the thought. Of course, it would be the usual free-for-all. Whose serial killer had more notches on his prosthesis, whose molester was more perverse, whose victim had more Facebook friends, whose perp was trending.

He wasn't putting himself out there: that's why the jobs were so scarce. He needed a new business card. Joseph Blumenfeld:

Bespoke Detective. Esquire? Nope, old hat. Your Boutique Agency for pop-up surveillance. For made-to-measure security solutions. For artisanal *what?*

Mugshots. Merch. Face on an eggwhisk, name on a golf umbrella. If your product won't move you may as well take your name off the door. Lie down on the carpet with a stick of chalk in your hand.

Then he thought about Valerie and the Littles. Davy, Sookie, Okefenokee and Lilo. What would become of them if he checked out? That greedy bastard Chief Detective Inspector Detective Chief Chief Culp had looted the Detectives' Provident Fund.

Hand in glove with the 101 set. He pictured them primping themselves for the Meet and Greet. Combing their hairpieces, holstering their deep-sea pencils, huffing on their smartphones and polishing them on the linings of their *what?*

He pictured them leaving their rooms. And just then the doors went *doef doef doef* like distant gunshots, the flat bark and so on. They thought they would see him in the Assembly Room. Think again.

Doef. That was Vermeulen. She would close one dyed-blonde hair in the crack of the door. Monitoring the perimeter. Smart cookie. He saw her adjusting her fringe, now one hair short, in the lift mirror.

Doef. Chief Inspector Connell of the Gorbals. Hanging the 'Do not disturb' sign on the handle of his door, flipping the one on his neighbour's so it read 'Make up the room'. Highland humour.

Connell would take the stairs, working on that paunch of his as usual. It's not the soft underbelly of crime that gets you, Savolainen always said, it's the hard overbelly of the law.

That crazy Finn! With his goofy bow ties and his bungee-jumping. Poking Connell with a long forefinger. He heard footsteps in the corridor, drawing closer, pausing, fading away. And it scared him.

Doef. The sultry Scarlozzi. She would make an entrance through the kitchen. It was one of the great escape routes, almost as good as the air-conditioning duct. Whether coming or going.

Going! I should get out now while there's still time, he thought. He hauled up the blinds and put his mouth close to the cold glass. Still breathing. That's something.

He paced out the distance from window to door. He looked at the blackboard square of night in the window frame and the chalky formulae of stars and neon.

Should I throw a chair through it? He saw himself for a split second in the shards, almost connected, before he fell away in pieces. Ice on asphalt.

Never mind the window, he should go through the door. There was nothing to stop him, except his own failings as a Detective, his foibles and frailties.

He remembered the invitation folded seven times in a fortune cookie. 101 Detectives: Sub-Saharan Africa. Be there! Bang. He remembered the names of the Organising Committee.

There's a pattern I'm missing, he thought. A pattern I'm missing. Or is there a pattern I'm missing? And then it struck him. A pattern.

I know none of them. Where is Wouter 'Nougat' Niedermayr? Where is Scarlozzi, L, MD? The pointless rigmarole of introduction. It doesn't add up.

He took the leaflet from the dresser. How toxic are you? He looked at the numbers scrawled across it in Blumenfeld's symptomatic hand.

He remembered riding the bus in from the airport alone. He remembered checking in alone. Is there a Detective in the house?

He dialled reception. While the phone rang he folded the leaflet in half precisely and ran his nails along the crease.

Let's say the whole thing is a set-up, he thought, an elaborate sting to do away with me. Sting-aling-aling, pal!

He folded the top corners down to the crease and pressed them flat. Half a question: anxious without cause?

No, anxious with cause. Plenty. I should get out while there's still time. Before they come for me.

Half of another problem: fatigued for no apparent reason? Less fatigued than depleted. He dropped the phone.

He looked again at the door. But still he did not move. He was thinking. Folding.

Is resolve a failing or a flaw? If I leave, who will finish the paperwork?

Who will wrap things up? He froze for a moment, for old times' sake.

He unfolded the wings precisely. There was still time to find the *what?*

He launched the pig towards the window. It flew into white space.

Make the right gesture. Try. That's what it bubbles down to.

I am accustomed to waiting. It comes with the territory.

He pictured a wee paper sandwich board: Joe Blumenfeld.

1 (one) Detective: Sub-Saharan Africa. Herringbones (Pty) Ltd.

It brought a lump to his eye.

And a tear to his throat.

A *what* in the snuffbox?

Make up the room.

He felt small.

And then.

But.

Exit Strategy

The corporate storyteller is having a bad day. She's spent the morning in her office on the 11th floor peering at the monitor, occasionally typing a line and deleting it, or standing at the window, back turned on the recitation pod, looking down into the square. She doesn't like the view and so the force with which it draws her to the window is all the more irritating. The square is a paved rectangle, to be precise, enclosed in a shopping mall and surrounded by restaurant terraces. She sees an arrangement of rooftops suggesting office parks, housing complexes and parking garages, and streets nearly devoid of life. No one walks around here if they can help it.

While she's been musing, the monitor has gone to sleep. In its inky depths she sees the outline of her head, a darker blot with a spiky crown. Her fingers creep over the keyboard like withered tendrils. Not yet thirty, she thinks grimly, and already as gnarled as an old vine. She badly needs a story for the quarterly meeting of the board, a parable to open proceedings and set the tone. Just a week after that it's the annual Green Day, which demands fresh and leafy input. Which aquifer will she draw it from?

She scoots her chair aside to face the white slab of the desktop. This paperless expanse, a mockery of a blank page, usually makes her long for clutter, for a glass paperweight with a daisy inside it and a tangle of paper clips, but today it's as refreshing to her eye as a block of ice. She rests her forearms on the desk, palms flat and fingers splayed, and then she sinks down in submission until her forehead touches the cool veneer.

Up and *down*. Might these be the poles of her narrative system, as they are of the corporate structure? The analysts say that verticality is over and done with, and today's corporations are horizontal, self-organising and contingent, but she sees no evidence of this. She has to get the basics right. Complications will follow, but they'll be manageable if they rest on a foundation that's firm and true. Yesterday she was reflecting on *in* and *out*, the day before on *big* and *small*, but today it's *up* and *down*.

The terms must appeal because of her circumstances, and her history and psychology must play their part. She wants to rise, not necessarily all the way to the top but closer, and here she is, with ten storeys below her and another ten above. Middling is a purgatory. Better right at the bottom than here. Hence the fascination of the basement.

A face surfaces in the milk of her memory just as her own surfaced in the ink of the screen. There's a story somewhere. Who's that again? A friend of a friend. Yes, it comes back to her. Dumisane. He developed an unusual phobia: he thought something was going to fall on him. Something would drop out of the sky, when he least expected it, and put a farcical end to his life. Where did this fear originate? Perhaps a pigeon shat on him in the playground on some long-forgotten schoolday. Nearly every fear and foible can be traced to the merciless battlefields of first and second break. It's made his life unbearable. In his apartment, with a blank ceiling overhead, his anxiety subsides, although ceilings and apartment blocks have also been known to collapse. Going out is an ordeal. He cannot take a step without looking up. He wants to see his ignominious fate approaching, even if he's unable to avoid it. And so he does get hurt, because he's always banging into things, and the bruises and skinned shins these accidents leave behind confirm that the universe means to do him harm. It's just a matter of time before he steps in front of a car.

Fact is, the corporate storyteller muses, and it makes the bristly nape of her exposed neck tingle, things do come out of the blue and kill people, famously Aeschylus, but ordinary folk too. She has several accounts in her notebook at home.

On a winter's day in 1989, for instance, Uwe Kramer was hurrying across a carpark in the middle of Vienna, hunched into his parka, eyes fixed on the icy cobbles, when a falling object struck his head and killed him outright. At first, the police thought he had been bludgeoned with a bronze statuette, a poorly made tabletop copy of Rodin's *Thinker*, an explanation encouraged by the proximity of the Kunsthistorisches Museum, where many such objects are on display. But the murder weapon turned out to be an agglomeration of human waste evacuated (so they deduced) from the toilet of an airliner and quick-frozen on its plunge through the atmosphere.

The corporate storyteller had been in her new position for a fortnight before she discovered that there was also a corporate poet. It was at a meeting of the Financial Management Committee and she was due to tell her first story.

The Chairman of the Committee had just called the meeting to order when a tall woman in a luminous gown appeared from behind the whiteboard and began to speak in lilting tones about the stormy seas of the futures markets and the vicissitudes of the trade winds on the floor of the bourse. It was not her voice that captivated, however, but the lovely movements of her hands. The members of the Committee were entranced. There was a lectern but the poet did not stand behind it. She prowled around the boardroom table and every head swivelled to follow her. With a flick of a finger, she launched one metaphor after another onto the hushed air, and when they had almost escaped her, caught them up again and drew them to her breast.

The corporate storyteller was appalled. She pictured the words squirming like small animals with their tails pinched between curved fingernails. To dispel this unhappy image, she fixed her attention on the poet's gown, through which she could see the curves of her hips and breasts. Was that a hairdo or a hat? Braids adorned with beads coiled about her head and fell to her shoulders, where they fused with her dress. A headpiece, the storyteller decided. It made the poet look lofty and prolific, as if her head was spilling sinuous verse. Although when the flow ceased, it was not words that echoed but gestures, a repertoire of movements of the hand and head as graceful and precise as any ballerina's.

When her turn at the lectern came, between a lively discussion of the risk appetite for the new quarter and the latest modifications to the regulatory framework on corporate governance, the storyteller could not find her stride. She felt like a cashier in her prosaic business suit. There was nothing wrong with the story. It was a post-industrial piece, using the outmoded mechanics of cogs and levers to describe digital processes. It was graphic, she thought; it let the listener see the lever in leveraging. But she did not deliver it well: the words pooled on the floor of her mouth. At the heart of the story was a drop of oil that greased the wheels, spreading itself ever more thinly over the entire mechanism and allowing it to function, a lyrical passage perfectly in keeping with the poet's contribution, and when she reached this point she glanced up at last from the screen to try to catch the poet's eye – but she was nowhere to be seen.

There were appreciative murmurs afterwards, but the storyteller knew that her first bolt had missed the mark. This dismal performance plunged her into anxiety about her new job. She had been headhunted by the corporation, or so she believed. When the agency's letter arrived, she had been working quite happily for a family concern. The package on offer was impressive and the personal approach was flattering. But how had it come about? She felt so uncomfortable in her new position, and so unwelcome, that she began to think some rival might have set her up for a fall.

In the weeks after her debut, she kept hoping she would bump into the poet, but she never did. That splendid, suede-booted personage made an appearance at board meetings and the occasional function, always slipping in at the last moment as if she had just been getting her make-up done in some fabled green room, and then she melted away again before the meeting was adjourned.

Finally, she'd asked Liselotte, the receptionist on floor 11, if she knew where the poet spent her working days. And so she learnt that her elusive colleague had an office somewhere above, on a higher floor. On 20, Liselotte said. Maybe even 21.

After that, she was never at ease in her own office, which everyone thought so stylishly spartan. She was in the wrong place, as simple as that. She belonged at a higher level.

The storyteller reached out to the poet once in her awkward way. At a special meeting of the Audit Committee, when the poet was still hovering, she tried a gesture herself, an undulating hand movement meant to convey the passage of time in a language her fellow artist would understand. But apparently her grasp of this language was poor, for one of the clerks in Strategy & Communication misunderstood entirely and came hurrying up to the lectern with a glass of water.

The recitation pod pings. It's a soft but insistent sound, an electronic throat-clearing like the chiming of her refrigerator at home when she forgets to close the door. It wants attention.

The storyteller lifts her head from the desk and sniffs the air like a savage. As always, the sound is accompanied by a pleasant smell. What is it this time? Cinnamon, cloves, caramelised sugar. The laboratory's idea of toffee apples.

The recitation pod repels her. How silly she must look standing in the corner of her office with her head in the hood, as the manual calls it. Like the classroom dunce. You cannot read in there, which is her forte. You can only speak. That's what it's designed for: to prevent you from reading and to teach you to speak. That's why Human Capital & Technology allocated it to her. It has been recorded under 'Number of training opportunities facilitated' in the Corporate Balanced Scorecard. The fact that she is a reader by inclination and training has been noted and evaluated, and registered as a fault to be corrected or rather a challenge to be overcome. Nonetheless, when she goes into the pod, she always holds an open book in her hands, her forbidden notebook. Otherwise her fingers keep rising to the hood and touching its cold surface. She even keeps her eyes downcast as if she can see through the armoured shell and its rubber lining and follow the words on a page.

It is red inside the hood most of the time, a dense, dusty maroon as suffocating as old theatre curtains. Sometimes the colour changes, for reasons she cannot explain, to a minty green or a spacious midnight blue, and then she feels as if she could learn to breathe in there. But just as suddenly some viscous shade of yellow will wash back in and suck the rubber lining to her skull.

Going in, thrusting her head through the puckered aperture under the bell of the hood, is bearable. The ruff, lying heavily on her shoulders, reminds her of the protective bib the dentist's assistant drapes over her when she's about to take X-rays. The unexpected heaviness of something that appears to be light is pleasantly confusing to the senses. She almost enjoys the dead weight pressing down on her shoulders.

Coming out is another matter. Sensing her intentions, the hood contracts around her head like a prodded anemone. She has to wrestle herself free.

After a month of treatments in the pod, each more combative than the last, she'd gone to the hairdresser and had her sleek hair cut short, and now she wears it in stiff, unruly spikes, a carefully styled disorder which her skirmishes with the hood cannot ruffle. The new look was meant to register her dissatisfaction, but it went unremarked.

Oleg was her sister's idea. The world is full of good men, Joan always says, jerking her chin towards the nearest window, but you must be open to meeting them. He's exactly your type.

He was new in town. She took him to a rooftop restaurant on the edge of the old business district. Climbing six gloomy flights of stairs, past floors cluttered with derelict knitting-machines, overlockers and steam presses, they emerged on a canopied island hung with ferns and orchids and paper lanterns. The furniture was spindly Scandinavian, the crockery eggshell Japanese. Oleg let her have the view: the grimy roofs and façades of factories and offices, chimneys and soot-stained windows, the overhead lines of the railway, the girders of a flyover, and here and there a rooftop café or club, bright and colourful islands like their own, where people like them were eating, drinking and flirting, elegantly suspended between heaven and earth. They ate vegan wraps and drank Chinese beer.

She did not like Oleg, but she was taken with his hat, a natty, multicoloured porkpie made of raffia. He had a fussy routine for adjusting its fit, which he performed every five minutes, raising it ever so slightly between the palms of both hands, with his sticky fingertips kept well clear of the pristine weave, then tilting the brim down over his forehead, before sliding it back onto the crown of his head and bedding it down a touch. He knew precisely where it sat best.

Oleg was a DJ. He travelled constantly, he told her, in search of new sounds. Last week he was in Sarajevo, this time next week he would be in Lubumbashi. After that maybe Bamako or Luanda or Cairo. Some of the best new sounds were in Africa. War zones did not frighten him. Some of the very best new sounds were in conflict areas. Kiev, Bristol, well not really. At the end of this itinerary, he adjusted his hat again and gazed over her shoulder into the jungly heart of the restaurant, cocking his head as if he was listening for new sounds in the foliage.

She looked in turn at the skyline over his shoulder and listened. She heard taxis hooting down below and scraps of talk and laughter carried on the breeze from the islands upwind.

What hat is he wearing now? she thought. What is he keeping under it?

He did not want to take it off, and ten minutes of teasing were needed before he let her try it on. She was sure he would be bald underneath, that the hair curling from under the brim was just a fringe, but his hair was as thick and glossy as a Labrador's.

The bond between hat and head was not easily restored. He repeated the routine three times before he was satisfied.

Is he scared of losing his head? she thought. She had learnt to see every human action as sign, symptom or subterfuge. It was one of the unpleasant side effects of being a storyteller.

She was reminded of a poet she had read about, a famous Swiss poet who wore a hat with a mechanical cuckoo that popped out through a trapdoor when he pressed a remote control. An eye-catching visual aid to embellish the punchline of a poem. She told Oleg about it, but he was not much interested. The sounds in Berne and Zürich were very thin, he said, because of the altitude and the democracy. Whereas the sounds in Reykjavik and Sofia were intriguing, despite the lack of conflict.

Raffish, she thought as he adjusted his hat again. Could it be related to raffia?

She saw afterwards that Oleg's manoeuvres had less to do with his hat than his hair, which had to sweep from under the brim in exactly the right devil-may-care way. The hat was an accessory for keeping his hair in place, like a hairpin or a comb, and he wielded it constantly as if someone was on the point of taking his picture. Perhaps it was an invitation.

If only she had changed her hairstyle sooner, she thought now, she and Oleg might have had more to talk about.

The storyteller fans the pages of her notebook under her nose to dispel the smell of apple pie (or whatever it's meant to be) and looks down on the familiar scene. The prefabricated geometry of the new city subdues her eye: the taxi rank, the corrugated canopy of the petrol station, the black coil of the freeway, office parks and townhouses, the skywalk to the convention centre, the rooftop parking at the mall, the fountain in the square. It's all strangely silent. Something so large and various should make a noise. A soft hubbub, rising up ten floors to her open window, would be reassuring. But the windows are sealed tight.

She remembers her father asleep on the sofa on a Saturday afternoon with the television playing mutely in a corner. Little men would be driving golfballs down green fairways: the balls rose in stately arcs and hung in the air so long it seemed the film had stopped. Silence took the sudden life out of things. Through the fluted legs of the coffee table she watched her father's chest to make sure it was rising and falling, her attention all that made him breathe.

Now she scours the streets for signs of life. Everything stilled, hushed, bleached to the bone. Yet there are more people than usual in the square with their faces turned to the sky. Heliotropes, she thinks, following the sun. Perhaps they see her here at the window and envy her the panoramic view, little knowing how it makes her feel.

If your office is higher up, you have access to the roof garden. There is no rule that says a data capturer from the 5th floor or a junior manager from the 9th cannot get into the lift and go up and sit in the sun eating a low-fat yoghurt or reading a report, but the fact is that no one from the lower half of the building ever does. A variable gravitational force keeps them in their place or draws them down to the lobby or the square. This force weakens as you rise. Nearly everyone on the top four or five floors sometimes goes up to the roof, even the PAs and receptionists. The people on the top floor pop up there every day. It's their territory.

She herself has been up to the 21st floor often, because that's where the boardrooms are, but she's never felt free to enjoy the view. Only once did she have time to imagine what it might be like to work there. Simonetta, the receptionist on floor 17, let Liselotte on floor 11 know that there was an unoccupied office in the Research & Information Department and so she went up in her lunch hour to take a look. It was a corner office with a clear view over all the surrounding blocks and it lifted her heart. The old city shimmered on the horizon like a mirage.

Her stories had improved by then. Though her performances were never as colourful as those of the corporate poet, they were steady and useful. At the Wellness Weekend workshop, she'd told the tale of Hiroto Yoshida, the marathon-running monk, and got more than the usual applause. Human Capital & Technology had even posted it on the intranet. She'd earned the right to make a small demand, she thought, and so she put in an application for a higher office.

She could not emphasise how much she loved the view. It would look as if she spent her time daydreaming, and even though that was part of her job description, strictly speaking, it did not seem wise to say so directly. She argued instead, persuasively she thought, for vision and perspective. Her current quarters were stuffy and constrained: she needed light and air and a more expansive view. She had to see the big picture. It was essential to her work.

Another ping. As she skirts the big white desk a savoury aroma wafts into her nostrils. Chicken soup? That's new. She sniffs all around the device. It's never given off such an intense fragrance. She's not sure exactly where it comes from, but she thinks it's a gland inside the hood.

She presses her palm to the shell. Hotter than usual too. Sometimes when it's hot to the touch it's cool inside. There's no telling. Especially when it radiates heat like this, it reminds her of an old-fashioned drier in a hairdressing salon.

It's been in her office for two months now. Human Capital & Technology keeps telling her she'll get the hang of it, but with every passing day she finds it harder to put her head into the thing. The thought of it sickens her.

On the advice of the Senior Manager: Knowledge Strategy, she's tried to think of it as a private retreat. It's supposed to be a learning opportunity: on-the-job training. But often when she's in there, she has the feeling she's being watched. The contents of her head are being extracted and processed. Someone is picking through this sludge to see whether she's been chewing properly. Input and output are topsy-turvy.

She cannot fathom its inner workings. The hood isn't large. From the outside it looks like you could hardly nod your head in there. But when you're in it, the space around you, laden as it is with dark shades, appears to be endless. Vistas open. Yet she chokes on the smell of the product in her hair and the synthetic exhalations from the hidden gland. She's tried reaching in under the ruff and pushing her hand through the aperture, but the rubbery collar clenches on her fingers as if it knows that her intentions are mischievous.

The manual is no help. It's full of advice about facilitating conversation with the intangible and honouring the work cycle by speaking your truth. You have to *speak* in there, that much is clear. The device gives your words weight and returns them to you, 'delivers' is the technical term, in an apparently tangible form. These returns are meant to be rewarding and to encourage further deposits.

But when she puts her head in it, she feels stifled. Her tongue lies in her mouth like a slug. Her jaw is numb and immobile. The words clot in the back of her throat.

No matter what it smells of around the pod – roses, candyfloss, mandarin oranges – inside it, one base note keeps striking through. Ammonia. It's like a well-scrubbed public toilet.

Her application for a higher office had got no response. A week passed without so much as an acknowledgement of receipt. She was on the point of writing again when Human Capital & Technology sent a clerk from Facilities Management & Maintenance to show her the office she could have if she wished to move. It was in the basement, on the third and lowest level of the parking garage, behind a metal door that looked as if it might conceal a generator or a switch box. But as the clerk had told her on the way down in the lift, it was the office occupied by the corporate storyteller in the days before that designation existed. The clerk was a skinny young man in a checked shirt and a long red necktie pointing downwards like an arrow on a graph. He unlocked the room with extravagant turns of several keys, reached in to put on a light and swung the door wide. Take your time, he said, I'll be back in half an hour.

It was a small, busy room with a fluorescent stripe in the middle of the ceiling and grey walls glistening with sweat. There were filing cabinets of a darker grey steel and a desk, shored up at either end by wire baskets marked *in* and *out*, both spilling papers. In a small clearing amid the papers lay a blotter with a calendar printed on it, the days of an unnamed month all but obliterated by jottings and doodles. Scattered like trash cans in a field of snow were cracked plastic containers full of paper clips, rubber bands, drawing pins, dust, lint and small twists of lead-blackened eraser rubber. A turned wooden vessel held some pencils with the paint chewed off their ends. The carriage of a typewriter jutted from a mound of crumpled papers.

The storyteller's heart soared. She rolled the chair away from the desk. It was something like a kitchen chair on four wheels with a leather seat cracked right through and caved in like a flopped sponge cake. She slumped down on it. It was the least comfortable chair she had ever sat on: the bumps and hollows left in the cushions by her distant precursor pressed into her flesh. It felt wonderful. She rocked for a moment in the chair, listening to its antiquated squeak and enjoying the painful pleasure of its anti-ergonomic grip, and then she tilted it back, gasping when it seemed to be going right over, laughed out loud when she found the tipping point and put her feet on the desk.

The wall before her was covered in books. Even the spaces between the books and the canted shelves had more books jammed into them on their sides. The rows under the ceiling leant in at a dizzy angle like a wall on crumbling foundations. It was a good thing there was no window. One stiff breeze, she thought, and the whole thing would topple.

The corporate fictions. She had never expected to see them. Bits and pieces had slipped through the online portal, crossing her screen in a flash, fewer and fewer of those as the techies had plugged the gaps. Just last week the Executive Manager: Strategy & Communication had told a meeting of the board that the corporate memory would soon be outsourced to a specialised company and accessible going forward only to senior staff members with the appropriate clearance. The sight of the corporate fictions, complete and unrestricted, overwhelmed her.

She rose from the chair and the sagging wall of books loomed over her. Any moment now, she thought, it will crumble and bury me. With a grim laugh, she prised a book from a shelf and opened it. A reference work of some kind, with rows of type in columns and a thumb index of golden letters on glossy black half-moons. She drew her forefinger down one of the columns and she fancied she could feel the rungs of type bumping against her fingertips. When she got to the bottom of the page, she lifted her thumb to the top of the next column, and then her fluttering fingers annoyed her, and she slammed the book shut and sat there with her hand in the trap. And that was how the clerk with the downward-trending tie found her when he came to fetch her back to the 11th floor.

I should have called their bluff, she thought later. I should have told them there and then: It's perfect! But it was a Friday afternoon and there was no apparent need to rush.

She spent the weekend strategising. Her application had been a model of suggestive thinking. The view from the window was hardly mentioned. Instead, she argued for being in the attic, in the head office, close to the limitless firmament of stories. Had the option been made available to her in good time, she might just as well have argued for being in the basement, with one foot in the underworld and the groundwater of myth seeping into the sole of her shoe. Perhaps she could now make a case for composing below and consulting above? Behind a closed door in the basement, she would be the corporate unconscious, left alone to ruminate and digest. And in her office on the 21st floor, in clear sight of the world, she would be the corporate conscience, approachable and consultative. Her door would always be open.

But she never got to argue the point. When she opened the door of her office on Monday morning, she was startled to find a technician at work inside. He was commissioning the recitation pod. She had never seen anything like it and yet she knew at once what it was for. The proportions of the hood and the foot-plate were unmistakable. The thing was made for a human head on a human body. The air smelt of burning leaves.

She tried to question the technician but he instructed her in a teacherly tone to sit at her desk and be quiet. She called Liselotte, but her old ally had already been briefed: Human Capital & Technology hoped she would make the best of this self-realisation opportunity. She was urged to navigate change by living out her personal destiny.

The technician finished tightening some bolts on the armature and stood back to inspect his work. He wiped his hands on a yellow cloth, and then he pressed his palms to the hood and massaged it gently. After a minute or two, he took his right hand from the surface and reached in through the aperture, while the left kept moving in small circles, rubbing and squeezing. Apparently he was satisfied, because he withdrew both hands with a smile. Then he quickly packed up his tools and went away without a glance in her direction. The device was silent. Only a bead of red light on the console suggested that it was live. Open for business, as she came to think of it.

The door had barely closed when the manual dropped into her inbox. The cover said 'User's Guide' in many different languages. Half the pages were devoted to numbered diagrams with arrows showing the placement and movement of head and limbs.

The drawing pin jitters across the desktop with a tinny hum, while the storyteller counts off the seconds on her stopwatch. The silver cap spins straight and true, as if eleven seconds are nothing, and then in a moment wobbles and cants and falls over. A pristine plane, she thinks, not a scratch, no blade, nib or compass point has come near it. Yet it leaches the momentum out of her top in an instant. The last of three tries, all short of the target. Now there's nothing for it.

She glances at the draft of her story on the screen, her new piece for the forthcoming quarterly board meeting. There's the title and the start of the first line. The Art of Falling, it says. And on a new line: It's been said that the art of falling . . . And that's all. Not a word more in three days.

She slips her feet out of her shoes and lines them up with her toes. She reaches into a drawer for the forbidden notebook. It's a pocketbook bound in soft brown leather. She opened it carefully when she bought it, starting with the flyleaves and peeling off pages at the front and the back in turn, pressing each one flat and running her thumb along the stitching at the spine, working her way methodically through the sections until she reached the centre spread. Then she numbered the pages in the top corner in pencil. The rest is blank.

She steps onto the footplate and crouches beneath the hood with the ruff over her shoulders. This is always the worst part: she must force herself to go on. An anticipatory hum sounds from the hollow above. She pushes her feet into the stirrups and straightens her knees until the top of her head touches the rubber. It smells like soup again, schmaltz and floury dumplings. Her scalp bristles as the hood begins to suck. She opens the notebook on the console, shuts her eyes and thrusts her head into the aperture.

Grey and damp. It's never been like this before. She feels shivery, light-headed, short of breath. Perhaps she's at high altitude? She would see far, over crags and precipices, if the mist lifted. Watery clouds envelop her, beading her eyelashes and flattening her hair against her scalp. She catches her breath, and breathes, deeply and slowly, trying to strain the smell of rotting leaves and disinfectant through her nostrils. When she opens her eyes again, she's drifting in the cloudscape. She floats over hilltops and it's almost pleasant. Once she tries to speak, but her jaw is locked. It's freezing up here, she thinks, and squeezes her elbows to her ribs. This reminds her of the book in her hands and reattaches her head to her body. She pictures the page curving like muscle from the spine, the goose-pimpled skin of the paper.

Who's that? A man at a window. A man in a black frock coat and a broad-brimmed hat. No, it's too vast to be a window: a wall of glass. He is rocking like a metronome.

She remembers. It's the transit lounge in Zürich. She's found a quiet annex, away from the crowds at the overpriced coffee counters and duty-free shops, where a trio of conjoined chairs faces the apron. She's dozing with her computer bag clasped to her side when a shadow flicks over her eyelids, coming and going like a pendulum. She peers through half-opened lashes. Near her a man has come to pray. He is swaying close to the sheer glass, which magnifies the outside world like an immense lens, blistered and veined with rainwater. On either side, gleaming fuselages are coupled to the concertina folds of gangways, but the bay in front of the praying man is empty. An expanse of wet tarmac stretches towards a hangar with its door gaping. This steel-framed black space is a gigantic version of the screen she spends her days gazing into. The man wears a hat with a tall crown and a saucer brim, perched high on his head, and he holds a book but never looks at it: the litany on his lips he knows by heart. His voice rises and falls, scattering dust on the polished veneers of the terminal. A remnant of old Europe in a costume out of a museum, perhaps not even a man but an automaton, bowing repeatedly to the void. Although she cannot understand a word, she hears a melody and counterpoint of resignation and protest. Half-asleep, entranced by the spindrift of his beard breaking on the lapels of his coat, she begins to mumble the prayer under her breath.

A memory stirs in her joints. She tries to follow the motion of the man in the hat, but the hood tightens its headlock. Instead of moving her torso, she moves her hips. The mist is audible, the words spurt from the man like air from a bellows and curl around her temples. A glow begins to rise under the hood and she smells rubber. She keeps on swaying her hips, scraping her shins against the calipers.

For a moment she pictures herself in the corner of her office with her head in the pod, but the image is unconvincing.

She closes the book on her forefinger, keeping the place, and presses the spine between her legs. As she sways, one strategic thrust after another chugs along the rosy membrane in capital letters, moving from right to left as resolutely as breaking news. Is she reading or writing? Is someone speaking? The stream reveals nothing. The pod owns the syntax, she thinks. Perhaps the vocabulary is mine, the soft, warm deliverables? She identifies inputs and outputs and aligns them with the mission statement, and then she manages them efficiently and effectively through the downswing and the uptick.

She would drift in the overproduction of pleasure, with the empty book squeezed between her thighs, but the pod loses interest abruptly. Sinking down on the footplate, she observes that the door of her office is still closed, thank God, and sits there rubbing her shins while her breathing slows.

The storyteller has her feet up on her ice-white desk. She wishes she could busy her hands with a smoke, although it's strictly forbidden and would set off the fire alarm. She laces her fingers behind her head instead. The light on the telephone has been blinking ever since she came out of the pod. It can wait.

She holds out her hands to see whether they're still trembling. She feels more like herself, but the office is as unfamiliar as a hotel room and the man in the hat bothers her. Where in God's name did he come from?

She looks again at the title of her new story on the screen: An

Unexpected Climax. Is it fit for a corporate fiction? That depends on whether it promotes the corporate vision. When it's done, she'll try it out on Simonetta, the receptionist on floor 17. Erotic fiction is her thing. Then the Equity Committee, Credit & Risk. One step at a time.

She runs through the first line in her head: They say that an unexpected climax ... And then she looks out of the window. Perhaps I'm not made for the storytelling racket, she thinks. I should find another occupation.

Just then, a camera pops up in the bottom of the window frame.

For a startled moment, she thinks it's a gun. Someone has been sent to kill her. This is how the corporation terminates your services; she's invited the chop with her lack of enthusiasm and resistance to self-improvement. But no, if she's being shot, it's only with a camera. The device drops out of sight briefly and then rises again with intent and she sees that it's attached to a human head. The head of a man. *Now*, she thinks.

The camera is rigged to a padded skullcap that elevates it slightly above the man's head. When he looks at her, it's like being looked at by two people. A camera crew.

She waves. She recognises the regal gesture as she's making it: it's the stiff-fingered, windscreen-wiper salute of modern royals. The motion you would make removing a grease spot from a mirror.

He cannot see her or has chosen to ignore her.

She gets up from the desk and goes closer. At the same time, he reaches up with one hand, hooks his fingertips into a channel on the window frame, twists his body and steps up with the opposite leg. Out there is the narrowest of ledges, hardly more than a lip on the frame, but he gains a toehold. Like a lizard on a garden wall, she thinks, as he clings crookedly to the glass.

She must be invisible to him, she's sure of it now, but she cannot accept it. She kneels down on the carpet so that her face is close to his, raises her right hand with the index finger pointing stiffly upwards and moves it from side to side. She recognises this gesture too: it's the movement her optometrist makes to check whether her eye muscles are working properly. There's an instrument for this purpose, a little mace topped with a shiny orb, but Mrs Jonas prefers to use her finger. Nothing.

She's spent every working day of the past eight months in this office, without once considering that one might not be able to see into it from outside. There's a bronze-tinted film on the glass that makes it seem as if sunset is never far off, and she likes the effect, it improves the atmosphere. Now it occurs to her that the film might be intended to ensure her privacy. But from whom? She looks down into the square inside the mall with new interest. More people than ever are crowded together there, and they all appear to be looking at her, although of course they're looking at the climber. In all the times she's been to the mall for her banking or her pedicure, or even when she sat at Armando's drinking a glass of sauvignon blanc, she never once thought to step out into the daylight and look up at her office. Somewhere along the line, without her even noticing, the flame of her curiosity has been snuffed.

The climber reaches up again and with another reptilian motion lifts his foot onto the ledge and stands upright against the glass. At rest there, arms and legs stretched wide, he is transformed into a fine specimen of a man. As good as a sketch by Da Vinci, she thinks, anatomically accurate and symbolically allusive. Vitruvian Man on his way to the gym. Not naked, mind you, far from it, sheathed from head to toe in some sort of leotard. A climbing suit, she imagines. An *extreme* climbing suit. Beneath the stretchy fabric, baggy at the knees and sweat-ringed in the armpits, he's slim and muscled, an athlete. A long face, sun-browned and attractively weather-beaten. Not a young man, she thinks, a man in his prime. Jets of sandy hair spurt through the air vents of the camera mount.

Oblivious to her presence. This authorises a closer inspection. Bending towards the glass like a museum visitor before a work of art, she examines his codpiece and the sculpted ridges on his torso. From close up, at least some of them appear to be made of plastic: he has a plate of body armour attached to his midriff. The pectorals and biceps are screen-printed on his suit. As he adjusts his stance on the ledge, she sees his own muscles flexing beneath the hard-edged outlines on the fabric.

A pouch of resin dangles from his belt. He reaches into it with one hand and then the other, and beats the excess off on his thighs. Then he leans back to assess the ledge on the 12th floor. The underside of his chin is an arrowhead. His calf muscles bulge and the printed versions amplify the effect. Any second now, he'll be gone.

She makes a fist to knock on the window. But what if she startles him and he falls? As she kneels there with her knuckles turned to the glass, there's a roll of thunder, and then a shadow flicks over the glass and the sound becomes the clatter of a helicopter.

The climber scuttles upwards. Just like a lizard, his asymmetrical hustle, but she thinks: The Human Fly. And she wishes this had not come into her head. At this moment, she has the feeling she's seen all this somewhere before. The man on the ledge, the woman in her office, the predatory helicopter circling. A movie probably. It's a distressing idea: this might be the most interesting thing that's ever happened to me, she thinks, and yet it feels like a cliché. Everything surprising has already happened before or is about to happen again. No matter what I do or say, or how I remember it or tell it, it will never be interesting enough. She presses her cheek to the glass and tries to catch a glimpse of a rubber sole, the elegant slipper of an acrobat, as the climber disappears from view.

The corridor is deserted. Closing the door softly behind her, she crosses the carpet on her bare feet, glancing through the open door and sealed window of each office she passes. She can hear the muted thud of the chopper, but all she sees is one tea-stained swatch of sky after another, like a strip of film with nothing on it.

Liselotte is not behind the half-moon desk in the reception area. Leaning over an arrangement of silk roses and baby's breath, the corporate storyteller glances into the blank monitor, just as a bubble breaks in the water dispenser.

In the silence that follows she hears a small uproar. It's coming from the conference room off the lift lobby, where a door stands ajar. They are all there, every rank and income bracket from the senior managers to the receptionists, hunched over the table with their fingers laced under their chins or perched on the armrests of chairs, eyes on the television screen, transfixed. A mutter of commentary. No one even looks up as she slips into the room.

When he was close enough to touch, she did not fully appreciate the climber's fancy dress. Seeing him now on the screen, magnified and distanced at once, she gathers that he's a bargain-basement superhero. He has red leggings and green briefs, and a yellow bandanna or scarf knotted at his throat, the suggestion of a cape. He's swiftly scaled another six floors. Three more to the top of the building.

A reception committee stands ready on the rooftop. It's like the end of a marathon: someone holding a towel emblazoned with the sponsor's logo, someone else proffering a bottle of water, a third person, invariably a man in a suit, ready to shake a hand and present a platitude. There are a dozen men in uniform too, security guards or policemen with truncheons and two-way radios.

The camera zooms in on the reception committee. That's the Chief Risk Officer. And the woman beside him? She bristles at the thought that it's the corporate poet, summoned to deliver an occasional poem, but it's Duduzile, the PA to the Operations Manager: Facilities Management & Maintenance. Almost as bad. The very woman who processed her request for a higher office. Her skirt flutters like a frantic bird in the downdraught of the rotor. Or it may just be the wind. It's always blustery up there, according to Simonetta, a sudden gust once blew the lettuce out of her salad. The edge is alarming too. She expected a barrier more imposing than this waist-high parapet and flimsy handrail. It shouldn't be so easy to step off into the void.

The climber can go no further. He pauses on the ledge of the 21st floor, holding on by his fingertips, and leans back to consider his final move. A policeman on the rooftop leans over to talk to him. Spiderman has a problem, she sees now. The channels in the window frames that he's been scaling end here. Above is a concrete overhang, wider than the ledge on which he's standing, and then nothing but the smooth face of the parapet. It looks unassailable. They could open a window and let him climb into one of the boardrooms – if the windows opened, that is. Surely he considered all this before he started his ascent?

No matter what his plans are, she knows this is the most dangerous part. She watched a documentary once on high-wire walkers and learnt that the truly risky moments in any act are stepping off and arriving back. Out in the middle of the wire, when the spectators' hearts are in their mouths, the artist is in perfect control. It cannot be otherwise. Balanced over the void, depending only on himself to defy the laws of gravity, his concentration must be pure. Every distraction is tuned out. But when he comes back to the grounded end of the wire, and must pass from his ethereal element into our earthbound one, he is most at risk of falling. The people who wait there, the assistants and seconds, even the most seasoned ones, have to stop themselves from reaching out to seize a hand or an arm. It's a natural instinct, this urge to drag someone to safety, but it must be resisted. The artist, who has put his life in peril, must be left alone to save it.

It's the same for this daredevil, she thinks. Here within reach of the summit, he is most likely to fall. There is no art to it either.

It's physics. He must have an exit strategy. Perhaps he and the policeman are discussing this very thing, as now both of them are shooing the helicopter away like a scavenging gull.

She sees a cameraman there, hanging out of the door of the craft in a harness, and realises that he cannot be generating the pictures she's watching on the screen, as she supposed. There are cameras elsewhere. Everywhere.

The pilot misunderstands the signals, he thinks they're summoning him, and the helicopter's nose dips and comes in closer. The climber clings to the glass with his little cape flickering. Any moment now he'll be peeled from the surface like a leaf and flung into space. On the rooftop people are waving and shouting into handsets. At last, the helicopter lifts up into the blue. The camera sees it off to a distance, and then turns back to the rooftop to show the main characters in close-up: the policeman at the railing, looking down, the climber on the ledge, looking up, and the Chief Risk Officer, looking ahead. The people in the square below, who are no longer the audience, have been forgotten.

The climber reaches into his resin bag with one hand and then the other, and rubs his thumbs over his fingertips as if he's thinking about money. Bracing his feet against the frame on either side, he scuttles up the glass to the top of the window. Then he reaches with his right hand for the ledge above.

The storyteller is back at her post. Ten minutes have passed while she waited for the man to fall past her window. Still nothing. The blades go on churning the air outside, but in here it is silent.

She jiggles the mouse to waken the monitor. Then she deletes the title and first line of her story and types: The Exit Strategy.

She considers the phrase. Every storyteller she knows has spun a tale out of it. Once it was a platitude in business and politics, now it's become a principle, a philosophy – one she should apply in her own life and work. You must know when to get out, when to disinvest, to sell, to liquidate, to terminate, to retrench and fire, to decommission, cut your losses, save your bacon.

It's beyond her job description to shut the computer down, but there's a power button on the monitor. She presses it and it collapses to black.

There are pens and pencils in her briefcase, clasped in elasticised loops like cartridges in a bandolier. She chooses a 3B pencil, opens her notebook to the first page and writes: Exit Strategy.

If everyone now requires an *exit strategy* – relationship counsellors, rugby coaches, foreign-policy makers, urban gardening experts, marketing managers, military commanders, surgeons – it's because the concept is crucial. The crux. Going in is nothing: pulling out is the hard part. You have to know how, why and when to put an end to things. To stop, cease, desist from.

What in God's name is that?

She goes quickly to the window. It's a handprint on the outside of the glass, a powdery impression of a palm, four fingers and a thumb. A left hand, she thinks, inverting the print in her mind. She sees him there again, crawling over her window. The good man. She raises her own left hand, thinking as she does so that it will not match, she's done this before or has seen it done, a failure of logic or imagination that led to disappointment. And it does not match. So she raises her right hand instead and presses it against the print, which it matches perfectly, and this consoling symmetry lifts her feet from the floor, she feels herself rising, going up.

Mountain Landscape

Dear Ms Williams,

re: Pierneef

Thank you for your letter of the 5th. I appreciate very much your ongoing involvement with the Company's collection, and especially your proposal for the redeployment of my Pierneef.

I read Prof. Keyser's article, which you kindly attached, with interest. It was thoughtful of you to highlight specific passages for my attention, and those were well chosen indeed, but I took it upon myself to study the entire paper. As you know, I have no particular knowledge of art, but Claudia Fischhoff, whom you might have come across in your dealings, is always encouraging me to educate myself. Claudia advises me on my modest private collection and has given me some valuable tips in the last few years. My only regret is that I started so late.

Your view that my Pierneef does not send the right sort of message about the Company is persuasively argued. However, I must take issue with certain of your conclusions. I hope you will humour me – and forgive the shortage of footnotes!

It may interest you to know that the painting in question was not hanging in the boardroom when I took over as CEO five years ago. Then the wall was graced by a photograph of Tokyo Sexwale and the lads of Free State Stars hoisting the league trophy. It was an appropriate choice for the boardroom – the Company's logo is all over the stadium – and I would have kept it, even though it doesn't quite measure up to the picture of Madiba in his springbok jersey at Ellis Park. But one day, not long after my appointment, I was browsing through our annual reports, familiarising myself with the corporate history, when I came across a photograph of my predecessor, Janus van Huyssteen, in front of a painting. And naturally I became curious as to its whereabouts.

I'm ashamed to say that I did not recognise a Pierneef in those days (you wouldn't catch me out now). I had to show the photo to Claudia and she brought me up to speed. She even photocopied a couple of things for me to read, just some facts and figures, nothing as penetrating as Prof. Keyser's article. Between you and me, I think Claudia had decided to take me under her wing.

The very next day, I set about looking for the missing Pierneef. At first I suspected someone might have walked off with it. A casualty of the transition. Fortunately, I thought to ask my personal assistant, Miss du Toit, who has had a long association with the Company. When in doubt, ask the secretary – another one of those things they don't teach you at Harvard Business School. Bless her, she remembered exactly when Mr van Huyssteen had the painting of mountains taken down and the photograph of soccer players put up instead. That dusty old thing! She pointed me towards a storeroom on the nineteenth floor and there it was, *Mountain Landscape*, jammed in between a filing cabinet and a three-legged chair, among piles of stationery and cleaning equipment. Nothing but mops, brushes and brooms. It would have made your hair stand on end to see everything jumbled together like that. There was a second canvas, a frisky little nude by Battiss, with the handle of a vacuum cleaner practically poking through it. A minor work, in my humble opinion. And some photographs of board members, and my predecessors at the helm of the

Company, not to mention some captains of the ship of state – but let's not go there, as they say. I had the Battiss hung in the reception area on the top floor, as a thank you to Miss du Toit, and the Pierneef brought up to the boardroom. (By the way, 'frisky' is Claudia's word, not mine.)

You may wonder why I did not think to ask *you* about my painting. That's exactly what I would do today, of course. But at the time I had no idea you were in charge of these things. I'm afraid my learning curve had not even begun to ascend.

I have spent some time looking at *Mountain Landscape*. Occasionally, I bring a cup of tea in here, turn my back on our much-envied city panorama, and simply gaze at that square of paint on canvas. There are golden foothills, soaring peaks in purple and mauve, storm clouds advancing or retreating. I get quite lost in it, in its wide open spaces, its 'echoing solitudes' (to quote Prof. Keyser). It is full of silence and grandeur (and this really is a phrase of my own). Afterwards, when I return to the present, to find that I've spilt tea in my saucer or dropped biscuit crumbs on the carpet, I feel as if I've been away to some high place where the air is purer. I feel quite refreshed. I cannot speak with authority – one day at the Louvre will hardly atone for a lifetime of ignorance – but I suspect that this capacity to refresh the senses and the spirit is one of the marks of great art.

I have also spent some time looking at other people looking at my painting. From my vantage point at the head of the conference table, I often see my colleagues' eyes grow misty as they stray to the wall over my shoulder. I think I can say that *Mountain Landscape* is a compelling work, that it commands attention, and not just by its location in the scheme of things. The attention of my board members was not nearly as prone to wander when the wall was occupied by Mr Sexwale and his players.

Without meaning to, I see I have made two arguments in favour of my Pierneef. Let me introduce a third by saying that I cannot agree with Prof. Keyser on the painting's style. I think it is the 'style' she refers to (you'll correct me if I'm wrong) when she says that the painting has a 'mannered, otherworldly quality' and that it 'denies the humanly specific in favour of a dehistoricised abstraction'. (My spellchecker does not approve of 'dehistoricised' but I've copied it down exactly.)

Just after *Mountain Landscape* was put back in the boardroom – the photograph of Tokyo is now on 'permanent loan' to the staff canteen – I had occasion to entertain Leo Mbola of Telkom. And the first thing he commented on was my painting. He said that he recognised the scene as part of the Winterberg range near Queenstown where he grew up. To Mr Mbola at least the painting captured a specific place rather than an abstract somewhere-or-other. He even offered to show it to me if I ever come down to Queenstown for a long weekend – and I might take him up on the offer. I know from the photocopies Claudia made me that Pierneef was fond of long, solitary trips in his car, simply taking the open road and stopping to paint whatever caught his fancy, but I have no idea whether he was ever in the vicinity of Queenstown. Is it important to know whether this mountain of his exists in the world? Would it change our appreciation of his art? I cannot say.

But I do wonder what kind of person Pierneef was. Did he strut about like a king or was he a simple man you would have walked straight past on the street? He certainly had a special way of seeing things. Perhaps he was a bit of a dreamer? Or a man of peculiar habits? On a business trip recently, I read something about Vincent van Gogh in one of those airline magazines. The name of the author would have come in useful now as a footnote. I suppose someone like Prof. Keyser is in the habit of storing up the bits and pieces one might need to argue the case for or against. There's a lesson for me. Anyway, this article said that Van Gogh was a coffee addict. Apparently he used to drink twenty-four cups of coffee a day. Can you imagine! If I have so much as an espresso after lunch, I know I'll be up half the night with my mind racing. Twenty-four cups! The journalist mentioned this fact in passing, as a mere curiosity, but I think it explains quite a lot about how Van Gogh saw the world, about his 'style'. If you look at *Starry Night*, for instance, and imagine that you've had twenty-four cups of coffee since breakfast, it doesn't seem so strange after all.

I am returning Prof. Keyser's article to you with this letter. It is a photocopy of your photocopy, which means that the parts you highlighted in red for my benefit now appear as grey speckles, whereas my highlights are in green. I have made some notes about this and that, which I won't go over here. But please look especially at the last page. Whereas you drew my attention to the point about 'dispossession', I wish to emphasise 'the proprietorial gaze', which occurs in the previous paragraph. This is the crux of the matter, I think.

Will you allow me one more anecdote? Last week, Eddie Khumbane of Spoornet dropped in to discuss some very interesting developments in the transport sector. We had met before in the conference environment, but this was his first visit to our HQ. It turns out he takes quite an interest in Pierneef – he had all the facts and figures you could ask for. So the two of us, rank amateurs but passionate ones, if I may say so, talked art when we should have been talking shop. You would be amused to know that he called *Mountain Landscape* a 'prime piece of real estate'. He stood there with his hands behind his back, gazing at the painting as if he owned it, and not just the painting but the mountains themselves, the lofty reaches of the Winterberg. You would have thought he'd read Prof. Keyser's article. If you could have seen him, I think you might agree that the impression made by *Mountain Landscape* is not at odds with our corporate culture.

All things considered, it seems to me that the Willie Bester street scene you had earmarked for the boardroom might be better suited to the lobby, the western wall I think, where it will catch every visitor's eye, and for the time being I'll keep the Pierneef here with me.

Sincerely,
(Signed) H.K. Khoza

PS According to Prof. Keyser, Pierneef could have learnt a thing or two from Joos de Momper. She says De Momper's *Great Mountain Landscape* (1623), majestic though it is, has paths twisting through it, and on those paths are beggars, hermits, horses and dogs, and their presence makes all the difference. I cannot say whether she is right, because I haven't seen the painting yet – I must still search for it on the internet. Have you come across this De Momper? He sounds like an Afrikaner, but as far as I know there were no Afrikaners in 1623.

Lullaby

I saw them at the airport, the woman and her young lover, but I would surely have forgotten them by now if everything had ended well. You know how it is: unhappy endings sharpen the memory. So many things snagged in my mind afterwards, details that would otherwise have slipped away in the torrent of experience that courses through each of us without leaving a trace. One of their suitcases had split during the flight and the baggage handlers had sealed it with yellow tape. It was an old-fashioned case, not the hard mussel-shell you're advised to use these days, a battered brown-leather carryall stuck with labels showing palm trees and hula skirts, like something out of *Casablanca*. The boy, the young man, wrestled it off the clanking conveyor and they laughed about the tape: the chevrons made it look like the scene of a crime. Their second bag went by, a backpack full of zippered pockets, clips and slings, and he chased after it, squealing with laughter again, and nearly knocked me over. The suitcase must be hers and the backpack his: luggage and gear. Two styles of travelling, two versions of the world. He tugged a wisp of red from the gaping case and pinned it with hooked thumbs across his hipbones, a lacy thong, barely there, and she snatched it away, pretending to be embarrassed, and buried it in her shoulder bag. Quite a bit older than him, I thought, but young enough to show those slivers of belly and back between T-shirt and sarong. Half the passengers were in Hawaiian shirts and Bermudas, signalling that their island holiday had already begun. The couple sharing my row had ordered G&Ts for lunch. In my suit, even without a tie, I felt like a grown-up among the kids, and it was a relief to get out of the terminal and into a taxi.

My hotel was on the edge of Grand Baie. I knew the Coconut Palm well, a comfortable, touristy place close to a good beach and half a dozen restaurants. The exclusive resorts are more beautiful, but what's the point when you're on your own? Mr Appadoo at reception greeted me by name and asked how the new range was moving. Little touches like this make you feel at home, whereas chocolates on the pillow and the bedclothes turned down remind you that you're not.

'You must join us for sundowners at the Sandbar,' Mr Appadoo said.

'Thanks but no thanks. I'd rather take a dip, clear my head.'

I was in no mood to break the ice with a gang of sun-deprived Europeans, self-basting Germans straight off their sunbeds, and Brits so pale they glow in the dark, all behaving like teenagers on a field trip. Been there, done that. They would let their hair and a few other things down before the evening was over. After the first free drink on the terrace there would be a string of others you had to pay for. Inevitably, someone would discover 'Dancing Queen' on the jukebox.

I went to my room, meaning to change for a swim, but an invitation card on the dressing table distracted me. It showed a cocktail glass with a tipsy straw and a stream of bubbles that spelt out *Willkommen! Bienvenue!* The cartoon had the same outmoded charm as the leather suitcase at the airport. I did not have to be in Floréal before noon the next day. Perhaps a drink would do me good. On an impulse, I changed into shorts and a T-shirt and headed for the bar.

The Sandbar was no more than a handful of wooden tables

under thatched umbrellas scattered along the beach wall. *Stehtische*, the Germans call them, tables for standing at. Stairs went down to the sand; the sea was as flat and blue as a swimming pool, and so close you could leave your sandals on the grass and hotfoot it across to the water. Harry the barman had a counter with a sea view so that he could double as lifeguard. He knew some moves with the cocktail shaker and some jokes about Tom Cruise. He remembered my name too.

A dozen people were swirling about under the umbrellas, moored to their drinks on the tables like boats to bollards. A spume of coconut butter and rum drifted downwind. The ice had not just broken but melted. In a rising tide of accented English the odd phrase of Italian or German bobbed like a cocktail olive or a lemon wedge. The whole place was charged with the reckless energy people from a cold climate generate when they feel the sun on their arms and sand between their toes.

The complimentary cocktail was an extravagant thing in a hollowed-out pineapple, mainly rum and strawberry juice, I thought, with melon balls afloat like mines. Looking for a quiet corner, I went onto the terrace beyond the last umbrella, and there I saw them again, the couple from the airport, sitting on the same side of a table in the lee of a windbreak, pressed together, looking out to sea. They had their faces turned to the afternoon sun and their backs to the noise. Her hand was on his neck, rubbing the bristles against the grain.

Nearly every coincidence has a dull explanation – the airline and hotel bookings had probably been packaged by some agency – and I was only mildly surprised to find that we were in the same hotel. I was curious though. On another day, I would have left them there alone, but I went closer. It was enough to hesitate on the edge of their privacy.

'Would you like to sit?' the woman asked.

'Are you sure? That's kind of you.'

They made place for me at the table by shifting apart, separating into two distinct people.

'I'm Martha from Rotterdam,' she said, putting out her hand. 'And this is my son Eckhart.'

'Eckie,' he said. The boy had a fierce handshake and a goofy smile. I imagine it matched the one I kept pasted to my face to cover my confusion. Mother and son? The possibility had not crossed my mind, but now the likeness seemed obvious. They had the same thick blond hair, the same full-lipped mouth. I introduced myself.

'Are you enjoying your holidays?' she asked.

'I've just arrived. On business rather than pleasure, I'm afraid, although you wouldn't think so to look at me.'

'You must have a bit of fun too.'

'Well, I'm going to reward myself with a weekend of loafing when the work is done.'

'What kind of work?'

'I'm in the rag trade, as we call it. Accessories mainly. We have a factory in Johannesburg, but some of our ranges are manufactured here.'

'Rag trade!' he burst out.

Almost everything I said made him laugh, a disconcerting high-pitched snort. I very soon began to wonder whether he wasn't a bit, well, *slow*. He was too bright-eyed for a man of eighteen or twenty. Twenty-two? The fact that I couldn't place his age seemed telling. He had a rough-and-ready masculinity, and he was drinking like an old pro and rolling his own cigarettes expertly from a packet of Drum. His chin was covered with stubble, his neck bulged from a white T-shirt – you could see he'd been working out – but his eyes were childishly innocent. He wouldn't sit still. He kept squirming around on the bench like a child who wants to go out and play. When he knocked over his drink, a fat pineapple like my own, he looked distraught. His lip actually quivered.

A bit slow, I thought, definitely. That would explain the easy physical warmth between them, the way he nuzzled at her neck and put his arm around her shoulders, left his hand to curl over her breast. And perhaps it also explained why she received these attentions with no sense of impropriety, of a boundary crossed or sanction violated.

Eckie went in search of a refill.

'And what do you do in real life?' I asked.

'Real life?'

'What business are you in?'

'Oh, we're just on holidays,' she said with a laugh that ran deeper than her son's. 'We travel together when we can.'

'Is this your first time here?'

'Yes, we found it on the internet. You've been before, I guess.'

'Often. I like to stop off on my way to Europe. I'm lucky to have a good excuse.'

'Then you must give us some advice about the beaches.'

'There are great places to snorkel. Do you dive at all?'

'She won't go in the water,' Eckie answered, coming up behind her.

'And he won't come out.'

'A water baby,' I said.

'Water baby!'

He put down a tub of Bombay mix and went back to the bar. I asked again what she did for a living, but she wanted to talk about the best places to snorkel, to eat crayfish, to buy presents. This is what holidaymakers do: they indulge themselves. They do not want to be reminded of home. When she asked how long I would be staying, I wondered if there was an invitation in the question. She had not mentioned a husband. I looked for a wedding ring and noticed that she wasn't wearing one.

The party grew as new arrivals checked in and guests came back from their outings. So many Germans, but also Scots,

Italians, Swedes. The very pale blondes all seemed to be wearing red cotton pants. The small talk and flirtatious laughter grew louder and hotter until it was a roaring bonfire.

Eckie scampered about, overexcited and glowing, talking to everyone, making a collection of new friends and swizzle sticks. But he could not keep away from her. Every few minutes, he would be back to lace his fingers into hers or lean against her. I liked her neck, the way the tendons showed under her skin as she turned her head, but when he rested his face in that brown curve I thought: impossible. She has a lover already. Metaphorically speaking. She loves the boy too much.

I had another drink, in a glass. The sun slid to the bottom of the sky like a sodden cherry. I was about to excuse myself, when a gust of music and laughter reached us from across the water. A catamaran was coming in, a beautiful white craft with sails furled, running on its engines. The coloured lights strung along the deck were luminous in the dusk, and in that charmed web small figures could be seen dancing. I recognised the *Parakeet.* I'd done this cruise once before, and I planned to do it again this time, when the work was out of the way. It was touristy, of course, a packaged day trip to one of the islets off the coast, but delightful too. They would moor the cat off a beach strewn with dead coral – it was like walking on bones – and the crew made a barbecue while you snorkelled and sunbathed, and then they fed you fruit and grilled fish and poured rum punch under jury-rigged canvas. Castaways with catering. Perfect.

When the *Parakeet* drew closer, the dancing became wilder, as if the day trippers wished to show the landlubbers how much fun they'd been having. The captain, a dreadlocked kid in a piratical headscarf, brought them close to the beach, almost in among the swimmers, and then swept out in a wide circle, extending the trip by five minutes, marketing his services. Even before they'd cast anchor, some of the more boisterous dancers plunged into the water and swam for the shore. The others milled around on the deck, showing off their sea legs, waiting to be ferried in on the dinghy bobbing at the stern.

A strange tension crackled between the new arrivals on the terrace and the old hands on the boat. The tourist's timescale is finely calibrated: a single day is the difference between innocence and experience. The people on the boat seemed browner, saltier, happier. We watched them with envy as the party at the Sandbar faltered. The catamaran had reminded a few among us that there were meals to eat and brochures to read, and they began drifting off. My thoughts turned to my plans for the next day. I said good-night to Martha and Eckie and went to my room.

I saw them again sooner than I expected: in the morning they were on the shuttle bus to Port Louis. They were heading down to Black River so that Eckie could go parasailing. Tomorrow, he said, they might do the catamaran cruise, and the day after that snorkelling. And then there was walking on the ocean floor in a diver's helmet. She caught my eye while he prattled on and quirked the corner of her mouth as if to say: humour him, he's young.

Nearly every seat was taken – tourists on the way to one attraction or another, I discovered as they swapped notes. In Triolet we picked up a housekeeper carrying a bucket full of brushes and a feather duster, and I felt a twinge of solidarity with this woman who also had a job to do. I was going to the factory in Floréal.

I sat behind Martha and Eckie on the bus. Something about the heat and the closeness, the sense of being confined among strangers, made me overly aware of their presence. It was almost as if I were seeing some magnified version of them. I remember looking at the sea chart of her freckled shoulders and the bite marks on the earpieces of her sunglasses. He was wearing a cap, and a tuft of hair like a shaving brush stuck out through the hole at the back. I imagined that the passenger behind me, a German woman who couldn't stop taking photographs, was paying the same exacting attention to the back of my head, watching an enlarged bead of sweat run down inside my collar.

Before long we fell into a drowsy silence. Even the German's shutter blinked and closed. On the long, straight road out of Triolet, Eckie's head dropped and jerked a couple of times, and then he leant over and laid his head on his mother's shoulder. She put her arm around him and drew him close. She let him sleep that way for half an hour, scarcely moving so as not to wake him.

When the bus stopped on the outskirts of Port Louis to let off the housekeeper, Eckie awoke with a start. Sleep had wiped the features of the man from him entirely: his face was as soft and round as a boy's. He stretched and yawned. Then we saw it. Perhaps he noticed it first or perhaps I drew his attention to it by leaning over the seat for a closer view. In any event, we looked at it together. On the soft, freckled flesh of his mother's shoulder, where his head had been resting, was a perfect impression of his ear. He cried out in amazed delight. She dipped her shoulder to see what was causing the excitement. It was strange. The shape of his ear, perfect in every ridge and whorl, seemed to have been carved on her body. She rubbed at it, as if she could smooth it into her skin like a dab of suntan lotion, but it persisted in clear relief. Soon everyone was admiring it and laughing, amused or intrigued. The blood rose in Martha's neck. I cannot say why, but this odd, displaced organ embarrassed her. I cannot explain my response either: my stomach heaved.

It took five minutes to fade away, slowly losing definition like a waxwork in the sun. Once the commotion had passed, Martha and Eckie began to joke and giggle quietly, both of them flushed and radiant. He kept running his fingertips over the carved skin, discovering his own flesh in hers, again and again. When the image was almost gone, he bent down to it and whispered a secret into her body.

Soon afterwards, they got out. I was relieved. I put aside the briefcase I'd been holding on my lap, stretched my legs into the empty space, and tried to think about other things.

You know that I saw them again. We haven't had the unhappy ending yet.

The following afternoon, I was reading on the verandah when I saw the *Parakeet* coming in. It was earlier than usual, but that only occurred to me afterwards. What struck me at the time was the silence. No reggae or chatter, just the chug of the engines and the passengers hunched on the deck. The simple explanations – bad weather, spoilt food – did not cross my mind. A dark stain in the air made me go to the railing and watch the boat come closer. It seemed to me to be lying heavily in the water. There were no showy zigzags or loops; it nosed straight in among the swimmers, the captain cut the engines, and his mate threw the anchor overboard.

Then a sound rose from the deep and flayed the skin from the backs of my hands. It was coming from a woman in the bow, and I saw that it was Martha, slumped over a bright, shrouded shape. Her cries broke into the sunlight one by one, ragged and raw, like creatures torn out of her on a hook.

All along the beach, people splashed out of the water, knees up, as if a fin had been spotted in the shallows. I saw Harry the barman running down to the boat.

The passengers came ashore. Some of them went away at once, others clung together on the beach, talking among themselves and then to the people getting up from their deckchairs and towels. Martha still sat in the bow with the captain beside her, weeping quietly now, while the sun clanged on every surface.

I should go and speak to her, I thought, comfort her. We've made a connection. But I couldn't face it.

When Harry came up to the hotel, I followed him to the Sandbar and found him pouring rum into a dozen glasses on a plastic tray. He told me the story. The *Parakeet* had anchored off Coral Point as usual. While the crew prepared lunch, the snorkellers did as they always do, floating out into the water at the end of the beach and letting themselves be carried back on the current. I remembered it myself: you hardly needed to swim, you just lay on the tide, drifting, suspended between two worlds, with the sun on your back and your face pressed through the surface of the water into another dimension. No one knew whether a sudden current had turned Eckie in under the boat or whether he'd decided to swim beneath it. He'd been caught in a tangle of lines between the hulls and drowned. By the time his absence was noticed, it was too late. The captain dived in and cut him loose, and they hauled him onto the beach and pumped his chest for an hour. Even after they'd gone on board and turned the boat towards home, they went on trying to make him breathe.

But what about Martha? I asked. Didn't she see that he was in trouble?

She was sleeping, Harry said. She had sat down in the shade against the dunes, watching Eckie in the water. I imagined him floating on the current, rolling over now and then to find her on the shore. 'Look at me! Look at me!' She stretched out with her head in the shade for a moment, she said, just for a moment, and she must have dozed off. When she awoke, the captain was already in the water with the knife in his hand and the boy's body dragging. She thought her son had been murdered.

The boy's body. I could not picture it. It was easier to imagine that this was a prank, that he would cast off the shroud of beach towels and jump up, squealing with laughter.

An ambulance came. Two men in floral shirts waited on the grass, while another in a white suit went down to the water's edge, stepping carefully so that sand did not get in his shoes. The captain and his mate brought Eckie's body ashore on a board and the other men put it in the ambulance. The captain carried Martha ashore in his arms like a child. Her silence was more appalling than her weeping. Everything fell into it.

I did not go to Blue Bay or anywhere else. I finished my work and in the evenings I sat on the verandah with a book on my knees. The *Parakeet* was anchored nearby. The newly arrived holidaymakers, unaware of its freight, and some of the old ones, eager to make the most of the time left to them, swam out to the boat and splashed around it. Behind the counter at the Sandbar, Harry went on cracking ice and slicing limes.

The overnight flight to Frankfurt was packed and I wished I was flying business class. The penny-pinching would have to stop. Watching the backpackers stuff their bags into the overhead bins, I wondered what Martha had made of Eckie's rucksack. Could she figure out where everything went? Perhaps the travel agent had sent someone to help her, a guide or counsellor. They must have trained professionals for a situation like this. Or a sister might have come to support her. Did she fly home with the body? What do they do with the coffin? It must go in the hold with the luggage.

The safety film unnerved me. 'In the unlikely event of a loss of pressure in the cabin, oxygen masks will drop down automatically from the panel above you.' I imagined what it would be like to face death here, the suffocating terror of it. The cartoon figures on the screen, mincing stiff-legged towards the emergency exits or reaching calmly for the dangling oxygen masks – 'Make sure your own mask is properly secured before you help children and others in need of assistance' – were meant to reassure. These beige dummies should be less alarming than actors, who were real people after all, but they had the opposite effect on me. They looked like zombies. Flight of the living dead.

I ate the little helping of Moroccan chicken with the little knife and fork. I drank two little bottles of chardonnay.

There was an empty seat a few rows back, and after the trays had been cleared away, I thought of moving for the elbow room, the chance to put my head down for an hour or two. I remembered those stories about passengers on doomed flights who swapped seats with a stranger and were miraculously saved when the plane went down. But what about the others who were saved by staying where they were? There was no story in that. And there was no lesson in it either. You lived or died. Luck could not save you, and neither could love.

As soon as the lights were dimmed, I covered myself with the baby blanket and tried to sleep, but I was too near the galley. People looking for water or whisky kept pushing through the curtain, bumping against my shoulder.

In the small hours, when I had begun to despair of sleeping at all, a voice reached me. It was a young mother in the row in front of me. She had an infant in a bassinet secured to the bulkhead. I'd noticed her earlier because she kept getting up to look into the crib, to adjust a blanket or run a hand over the child's head. Now she was singing a lullaby. I did not recognise the language, but I understood it well enough.

The cabin was quiet. Under the lit signs that said 'Do not smoke' and 'Keep your seatbelt fastened' nearly everyone was asleep. The baby was sleeping, but its mother went on singing. Just as she needed to reach out and stroke the edge of the crib with her fingers, she needed to reach out with words into the soft shell of his ear. For a moment, I saw an aeroplane full of little children asleep in their adult bodies, under youthful muscle and middle-aged fat, behind beards and breasts. Babies. The long, grey nursery droned into the dark. I pulled the blanket up to my chin and the consoling babble washed through me.

Industrial Theatre

I

I don't know much about industrial theatre. To tell the truth, I didn't even know it existed until my friend Natalie invited me to the launch of the new Ford Kafka. In her younger days, Natalie was a cabaret artist, but lately she has made a name for herself on the industrial stage. She thought this particular performance would appeal to me, because I am interested in both reading and motoring.

As a special guest of Natalie, entering through the stage door so to speak, I would not be receiving an official invitation. But she showed me the one she had saved for her portfolio: a key ring with an ignition key and an immobiliser jack dangling from it. It was very much like the real thing, except that the immobiliser was embossed with a K. The details of the launch – venue, time, dress code ('black tie or traditional') – were printed on the plastic tag. I learnt afterwards that messengers dressed as racing drivers had delivered the invitations by hand to each of the invited guests. The trend in these things, says Natalie, is towards the extreme. Even the habitués of industrial theatre grow weary of cheese and wine and complimentary gifts, and something out of the ordinary must be proffered to reawaken their appetites. Then the hope is always that these custom-made playthings will lie about on desks and coffee tables long after the event and become talking points.

The invitation-key promised that our reception would be lavish. Yet, in my unsuspecting way, I was surprised by the venue. The Industrial Arena was not a makeshift stage in some factory or warehouse, but a convention centre on the outskirts of the city, just beside the motorway, with its own squash courts, a miniature golf course, and facilities for simultaneous translation. I had to leave my car in a parking lot and take a shuttle bus to the main complex.

The bare concrete façade of the banqueting hall, where I had been conveyed along with several other guests, reminded me again of a factory. But once I had made my way up an angular ramp and passed through some sliding doors, I found myself in a luxurious lobby, with carpets underfoot and chandeliers overhead.

Apparently I was early, for the place was nearly empty (six for six thirty, the invitation said). Near the entrance was a long table laden with glasses and I went hopefully towards it. A waitress handed me a brimming champagne flute. Another woman shook my hand and bade me welcome. A third ushered me towards a desk, where the early arrivals were having their names ticked off on a list, and I joined the end of a short queue.

I felt a flutter of panic when I saw the same black key ring dangling from three different forefingers in the queue ahead of me. What if Natalie had forgotten to notify them about our special arrangement? But there was no need to worry. My name was soon located on the list and my table pointed out to me on a seating plan. I went on into the hall.

All around me table tops floated like pale rafts on a dark sea. In the centre of each was a tower supporting a candle and a number. Here and there, a figure submerged in shadow clung to the edge of a table. I passed between them, repeating my own number to myself under my breath.

My place was in a corner near the emergency exit. It was as far away from the stage, an empty space flanked by loudspeakers and overhung by lights on metal bars, as it was possible to be. A card with my name on it indicated that the seat reserved for me was the worst in the house: if I sat here, I would have my back to the action. I quickly switched my card with that of a Mr Madondo on the opposite side of the table. Though I was now fractionally further away, I would at least enjoy a comfortable view.

On the seat of my chair lay a goodie bag containing several items of commemorative clothing, a sticker for attaching a licence disc to the windscreen, a sheet of plastic, and some booklets about the new Ford Kafka. The compilers of these publications had evidently been forbidden to depict the product, for there were no photographs at all, only glossy black rectangles and squares.

I turned my attention to the table decorations. The centrepieces proved to be parts of engines, artfully arranged with indigenous fruits and gourds, and proteas and veldgrasses spray-painted black.

The first course stood ready to be consumed: a number of pink shrimps curled up in a nest of alfalfa sprouts. Good manners required that I wait until all my dinner partners were seated. But then Mr and Mrs Rosen arrived, introduced themselves, tucked their napkins into their collars and began to eat. I followed their example. More and more guests appeared. Some opened their goodie bags as eagerly as children, others stored them under their seats without a glance. The air was filled with the clinking of cutlery on china, waiters began to circulate with wine, and soon the seats to the left and right of me were also occupied – Dr and Mrs Immelman, Ms Leone Paterson, Mr Bruintjies. Mr Madondo, whose place I had usurped, seemed not at all bothered by his situation, and my conscience was clear.

Despite our head start, Dr Immelman was the first to finish and, flinging down his fork, he challenged me to a conversation. Only then, when he stared at my lapel, did I realise that all the others were wearing badges with their names on them. However, that was the only uniformity I could discern. Mr Madondo was clad in a well-tailored tux, for instance, whereas Dr Immelman, in the name of the 'traditional', had gone for a khaki lounge suit and a hunter's hat. I asked about the badges. There was a table in the lobby, Dr Immelman said, where they had to be collected. Being new at the game, I had failed to notice it. I rose to rectify the omission – a badge with my name on it would be a far more desirable memento of the evening than any number of T-shirts and caps – but just then the stage lights dimmed, ominous music welled out of the loudspeakers, and the show began.

II

Midnight in Bohemia. In the distance, the silhouette of a castle on a rocky outcrop. At its foot, scraps of alleys and squares, the ruined pergolas of roadside inns, islands of cobble in rivers of shadow. On one of these moonlit islands, some lucky survivors, down at heel and pale as corpses, are trudging endlessly up a single stair. On another, a solitary girl lies writhing. Meanwhile, a boy in striped pyjamas confirms the dimensions of an invisible cell with the palms of his hands.

Then a droning undercurrent in the music surges to the surface. Driven aloft by this sound, a dozen narrow columns begin to rise from the floor. On top of each column a limp figure lies supine, limbs dangling, like a sacrificial victim upon an altar.

Natalie had intimated that Kafka himself would put in an appearance and that this pivotal role might be played by a woman. I was sure she meant herself, but her tone warned me to postpone my surprise for the forthcoming launch, and so I probed no further. Now something in the attitude of the victims, with their bulging middles and bulbous joints, reminded me of her. They looked as if they had been fattened on purpose. I climbed up on my chair – several other guests had already discovered this singular advantage of being at the back – and trained my opera glasses on each of the figures in turn. Their shins and forearms were encased in shiny armour, their knees and elbows in quilted pads. They had round faces and thickly padded bellies. Though I pried at the edges of their shells, I failed to uncover familiar flesh.

The columns continued to rise, each attaining its proper height at its own pace, until it became apparent that they were ranged in two rows to form a colonnade, tapering away towards the backdrop. Just as the last one reached the limits of its extension beneath the stage lights, the droning rose to a pitch of intensity. Crockery rattled and lights flickered. And then the outcrop burst apart, with a crash of cymbals and drums, and a cloud of mist boiled out. For a moment, there was nothing to be seen but furious red light and roiling cloud, nothing to be heard but thundering drums and bleating trumpets. Then an object issued from the crack, and though it was no more than a shape in the mist, charged with pent-up velocity by the laws of diminishing perspective, we knew with certainty that it must be the new Ford Kafka. Upon a narrow ramp it advanced, while elemental forces twisted and turned all around.

It was just as well that Natalie had enlightened me on the difference between industrial theatre and the conventional kind, or I should not have known what to make of this disconcerting excess of effects. Industrial theatre, she said, is not drama but spectacle. Its point is not character but action. And the only action of real import is the climax. There are peaks and troughs, it's true, but the troughs are short and shallow, and their sole purpose is to separate one peak from another.

To my relief, we now entered such a trough. Figures appeared suddenly with carnival music trailing after them like scarves. A party of young men and women went by, arm in arm. Chinese lanterns glimmered in the chestnut trees. Someone whistled in the dark. A spotlight pointed out an opening and a descending staircase, which technical wizardry had caused to appear in the floor, and the young people walked down it, laughing and talking, sinking away into the underworld. The lanterns swayed on the boughs, fragments of bandstands came and went on a damp wall. Another spotlight played across the shattered castle. Then that beam was broken too by a girl on a trapeze, who flew down from the moon and swooped over our heads, reaching out with one slender arm to catch us up – and missed – and vanished into the darkness.

On the ramp, in the barred shadows of the colonnade, the new Ford Kafka had begun to revolve, metamorphosing by painful degrees into another object. It was long and hooked at one end: that would be the bonnet, curving downwards like a beak. At the other end it was blunt, as if its tail had been lopped by a carving knife. I thought I recognised what the booklets in my goodie bag called the 'unique Kafka profile'. And yet it still wasn't clear, it was out of focus, like something wrapped in gauze. This lack of definition made it menacing.

As if to confirm my misgivings, the atmosphere thickened, the music took on a shriller tone, and another peak imposed itself. A pencil-thin spotlight slid down out of the gods and prodded one sacrificial victim, and then another, stirring them into action. One by one, they raised their stiff arms and legs, and scratched at the hot air. That was Natalie at the back, I would swear on it, enormously enlarged by a trick of the light, and quivering to beat the band. The spotlight kept poking and jabbing, like a stick in an anthill, until the stage was in an uproar.

The chirping and chafing reached a crescendo, and trailed off into a grey silence. In a distant corner an archway opened, and a lamp winked within, grew brighter, drew closer. A gondola floated out into the gloom. In the stern stood Death, in a cloak of sorrow. And in the bow stood Kafka, in a trenchcoat and a broad-brimmed hat, with the shadow of Death upon him, gazing unblinkingly ahead.

It was a mistake to use a woman, I told Natalie afterwards. And not just because she plays a socialite in that comedy on TV. It involved too much covering up. The stubbled chin was lifelike, I admit, and the ears were right. But the hat was only there to hold her curls and the coat to flatten out her curves. What was the point? They should have found some scrawny boy, with the right dash of Malay blood, and put him in his shirtsleeves, or a vest to show some ribs. Let him shiver!

The gondola bearing our disappointing Kafka rolled onwards, unable to change a thing about itself, but effecting a magnificent transformation in its wake. Spring-loaded thorn trees sprang upright, a ballooning sun rose to the end of its tether, the mist dissolved. Leopards and impalas and monkeys skipped out of the cardboard bushveld. The victims came out of their shells too, as the sacrificial columns sank down to earth, and joined the dance of life. There was Natalie, unfurling her wings.

While the bushveld bloomed, the gondola bearing Kafka arrived at the last remnant of Prague, a sooty archway in another distant corner, and passed through unhindered, dragging away the tail end of the twilight. When the steersman snuffed his lamp, the parade of the wild animals began. It was a relief to find oneself back in Africa.

Yet this is not the summit either! The show goes on. The animals prance, and pose, and prance again, and depart. The new Ford Kafka remains at centre stage. The revolving platform has restored it to its original shape, levelled at us. For some time, it stands there without moving. Then the platform tilts and the car rolls off it, bursting through its wrapping into a state of gleaming certitude, bearing down upon us. Those at the back feel safe, of course, but some in the ringside seats start up in alarm. Then we all see that we have no reason to be afraid, there is a young man at the wheel, smiling pleasantly and waving, and he guides the car expertly between the tables. He is an actor too, Natalie says, and made a name for himself playing a political prisoner.

It was a daring bit of casting, even by today's standards. In the passenger seat, letting her hair down and tossing away the hat, so that we cannot fail to identify her, is our Kafka. Now that I see her properly, I recognise her from the TV. At the sight of her plump cheeks, I imagine Kafka, in the final days of his consumption, and my heart goes out to him.

The car comes to a halt in our midst and everyone has to get up to see what's happening, creating the impression of a standing ovation. At which point the lights come up and the waiters move in with the main course: beef.

III

The most remarkable thing about the new Ford Kafka, as I discovered when I took a closer look at it after the dessert, was that it was not black, as I had supposed, but blue. Midnight blue, Mr Bruintjies said. Even the puffiness of the leather seats, which I had never seen the likes of before, was apparently quite normal, just another 'style'. I walked around the vehicle several times, but failed to find it as impressive as I'd hoped. I even queued to sit behind the wheel. It smelt good, I confess; it smelt healthy and prosperous. I breathed in the aroma, twiddled a few buttons, expecting something unpleasant to happen. And then all at once I was seized by the language of the motoring press. The bucket seat embraced me assertively. The gear lever became stubby and direct. The dashboard looked clean, the instrumentation unfussy. Gazing through the windscreen, I found that the bonnet had lost its Semitic curve and now looked nothing but businesslike. I gripped the steering wheel in the requisite ten-past-two formation. Or was it the five-past-one? What do I care? I could have sat there forever, with the Kafka logo floating between my wrists. But the queue was restless.

When I returned to my seat, an informal atmosphere had settled over the table. Mr Rosen had taken off his jacket, unselfconsciously exposing a pot belly and braces, and put on his commemorative cap, with the peak turned to the back. Mr Madondo was wearing Dr Immelman's hat. Apropos of the leopard-skin band, Mr Madondo declared that the next time the invitation said 'traditional' he was going to come in skins. Everyone laughed. There followed a diverting discussion about the value of tradition. After a while, I steered the conversation back to the new Ford Kafka – I was keen to get my companions' impressions. Mr Bruintjies was the dark horse: so great was his admiration for the marque, he had ordered the new model months before, sight unseen. It also emerged that Ms Leone Paterson had designed some aspect of the invitation-key, and she promised to send me one 'for my portfolio'.

I was by no means the first to leave. I had passed a pleasant evening, as I assured the company when we parted. But the moment I was alone, a mood of tense despair descended upon me.

In the lobby, heading for the shuttle bus, I remembered the lapel badges. The table was against the wall near the cloakrooms. There were several dozen badges no one had collected, a roll call of the missing – a Mr Ringwood, a Mrs Foote, me. And yet here I was, as large as life, a walking contradiction. On an impulse I swept the badges into my goodie bag and hurried away.

One day, the opportunity to test-drive the new Ford Kafka might present itself; for the time being, I will have to make do with a second-hand Mazda Midge. Before driving off, I took out a handful of the lapel badges and studied them again. Whereas the new Ford Kafka has a reading-light in the ceiling just like an aeroplane, the Mazda Midge has a little bulb you can hardly read a map by. I could make out Mr and Mrs Granger, a Mrs A. Chopho, a B. Capstine, a Mulligan. Unknown factors. Kafka's face, looking back at me from every badge, should have been a consolation. And yet it was as strange, as remote and inhuman in its familiarity, as Colonel Sanders.

I took the M1 South. As soon as I found myself in the fast lane, I began to speed. I wound down the window so that the wind could tear through me and pressed the accelerator flat. There was music in my head, a relentless droning I had never heard before but knew by heart, the soundtrack of industrial theatre. I let the car float to the left of the lane until the wheels on that side were thumping over the catseyes on the dotted line, and this gave the music a driving rhythm and made me go even faster. The towers of Johannesburg rushed closer. I drifted, I could hardly remember it afterwards, and all the time I was turning the names of the absentees over in my mind, as if they were members of one broken family, and wondering what, if anything, could be done about them.

Dead Letters

NEVILLE LISTER

Neville Lister, b. 1962, Johannesburg. Commercial photographer (mainly advertising: 'nation-building epics', magazine features, property portfolios). Recently some exhibited work. Contact: Claudia Fischhoff, Pollak Gallery, Johannesburg

Neville Lister grew up in Johannesburg and studied at the University of the Witwatersrand without completing a degree. He left South Africa in the early 1980s and lived for a decade in London, where he began his photographic career as a location scout. After assignments for department-store catalogues, property portfolios and 'everything in between', he found a niche in the women's magazine market.

Soon after South Africa's first democratic election in 1994, Lister returned to Johannesburg to pursue his commercial work. In the early 2000s, he began to photograph on his own account, although it was some years before he exhibited or attracted critical attention. His photographs of walls appeared in the *Public][Private* group show at the Switch Box in 2008; and his Thresholder series, portraits of people with their letterboxes, was shown at the Pollak Gallery the following year. At this time, he was mentored by renowned photographer Saul Auerbach.

Lister's current project involves a cache of undelivered letters that once belonged to a Dr Pinheiro, a medical doctor who sought refuge in South Africa after the 1975 revolution in Mozambique. Unable to practise without the proper certification, Dr Pinheiro found work in the sorting room at Johannesburg's Jeppe Street Post Office. Here he came into possession of the 'dead letters', various items of mail intended for people in the city but never delivered because the addresses were incomplete or indecipherable. Lister acquired the letters in turn shortly after his relocation from London. For many years, he was unsure what to make of them and could not bring himself to open the envelopes.

In 2010, while scouting for one of his Thresholder photos in downtown Johannesburg, Lister was attacked and robbed of his camera. The thugs strangled him and left him lying unconscious in the street with his pockets turned inside out. In an account of the incident, he writes: 'I remember fading to black; and I remember coming round again, sprawled under a blue sky, amazed to be alive. I am troubled by the derangement of consciousness I experienced in these moments: random images flickered through my mind like slides falling through a broken carousel or letters through a slot. People say your past flashes before your eyes at the point of death and perhaps this is what they mean, except that I was not dying but coming back to life. The light was blinding.'

A few months later, Lister began opening the dead letters. Reading these messages from the past and taking them back to the people who wrote them has become his admittedly quixotic mission. He has made several journeys in search of the far-flung return addresses on the letters. The people who posted them, thirty years ago and more, are long gone, but the journeys are a distraction and photographing the places is consoling. Transcriptions of five of the dead letters are presented here. The original letters and Lister's photographs of locations associated with them were exhibited in Kraków in 2011 (see 'Dead Letter Gallery').

Fixing a chaotic moment is Lister's 'speciality' as a photographer. He is known to his colleagues as 'Mr Frosty'. In April 2009, he explained this nickname to a journalist: 'The joke is that I'm known in the industry as the frozen-moment guy. You know, the moment when things teeter, when they hover and vibrate, just before the fall. Capturing it in the real world is no longer a job for a photographer. Anyone can freeze an instant digitally and tinker with it and thaw it out again . . . When it comes to these things, I'm like some old geezer who insists on writing with a pencil. I'm no Luddite, I appreciate the technology; it's just not for me. I still want to stage it all, to set up something foolishly complicated and get it on film, hoping for a small, unlikely miracle.'

Letter 1

L.S. to Maryvonne, 1978, Paris (tr. from French)

17, rue Boulard, 75014 PARIS   September, 1978

My dear Maryvonne,

I worry about you! The news reaching us from S. Africa is not good. On Sunday when I came back from Jean-Richard in Auxerre I saw the most terrible thing on television. I was so upset I phoned J-R at once, although we had only just been together. To see a man doused with gasoline and burnt alive, and no one lifting a finger to prevent it, and all for being black. Or is it some other reason? You must write again and tell us what is happening, especially with you. J-R and everyone else in Auxerre are worried sick.

Your last letter troubled me. What is the meaning of this fancy dress? I understand, I think, that you must go to dangerous places because of your work. I am the first to say that the research is important. But that you should go about in disguise, dressed as a man, as a black man, seems strange to me. Surely a minstrel costume is more likely to get you into trouble than to protect you? Who are you hiding from? And who are the comrades you mention? I believe that Orlando is in Soweto. I told J-R it makes me think of Orlando Furioso and he said he doubted very much they had heard of Ariosto where you are.

You always tell me not to sound like a professor, but that's who I am. And to me you will always be a student, even after your habilitation, please God! In any event, sounding like a professor is one of the few benefits of the job, so here goes. Picturing you with your face painted black (is this really what you do? – it seems so strange) I was reminded of the episode in Homer where Ulysses creeps into Troy disguised as a slave. Helen tells the story to Telemachus, who is looking for news of his father. Does it come back to you? No half measures for Ulysses: he beats himself black and blue, he takes the lash to his own back until the blood seeps through his filthy rags, he pounds bruises into his cheeks. Then he skulks through the streets of the enemy city. The disguise is a good one. Apart from Helen, who says nothing, not a soul recognises him.

It's a remarkable story, not so? But that's enough of the Ancients. When I hear from you, I will write again to say what I mean by it. Please be careful. Perhaps you should think about coming back to Paris for the summer. Maude says you can stay with her. You will always have a home here.

Your affectionate teacher and worried friend,

[Signed] L. S.

Letter 2

M. Benadie to Basil, 1979, Laingsburg (tr. from Afrikaans)

Oct 1979
Dear Basil,

How is life in the Golden City? I have phoned repeatedly, but no one answers.

Last Thursday an alarming thing happened. You remember I said I would dig a fishpond in the backyard as soon as I moved in? Well, I finally started. A whole year has flown past because I am always busy in the shop. I had just started when Mrs Greyling from next door came and said I shouldn't just dig holes like that. I said why, and she said well, certain things that cannot be named are buried in that yard and should rather be left undisturbed.

I thought she was pulling my leg but she said no, it was serious, and she showed me the map you drew when you went to PE on holiday and she had to look after your (i.e. my) house. She said every X was a nameless thing that had to be pointed out if anything unpleasant ever happened to you, like an accident or a drowning, and she was left behind to take care of everything.

Now there is a rockery that does not appear on your map. There is hardly room for a fishpond or a septic tank, which will also have to be rebuilt one of these fine days, another thing you should actually have drawn to my attention before I bought the house. In any case, please confirm that it is safe to dig here at the back or phone me rather (your old number) in the evening, because in this day and age it's better to write nothing down.

Please write back soon.

Yours sincerely,

M. Benadie

Letter 3

Karl-Heinz to Norman, 1977, Göttingen (orig. in English)

Geiststrasse 7A
3400 Göttingen
Wed., April 13th '77

Dear Norman,

Greetings from Göttingen! I hope this finds you well. I myself have settled in nicely here and am going on well with my work. As you can imagine, there are scholars galore to pore over Kant & Co., but very few with an interest in Netterberg. Indeed, my passion in this direction may be sui generis. It is all to the good: I am left to my own devices and getting ahead by dint of sheer provincialism.

Some weeks ago at the Bahnhof, which is a splendid place dating from the heyday of the Railways, I saw something that would have amused you. An old man, a shabby fellow with a brown cordroy hat like a mushroom squashed down on his head, was causing a rumpus on the concourse where the schedules are displayed. He was wandering among the commuters, almost as though he were sedated, I would say, and declaring to no-one in particular, but very distinctly, in well-accented English – 'I am the Brain Man of the World!'

I am writing on a different matter though. Please don't think me presumptuous, but when this question arose I immediately thought of consulting you. There is a story attached. My friend Adelheit recently took lodgings with a colleague from the University library. Arrangements of this kind are common here where space is at a premium. When she was cleaning the little refrigerator in her room, she came across a spool of film in the crisper. Apparently it is common practice to put film in the fridge to keep it 'fresh'. Her colleague surmises that it was left behind by the previous occupant of the room, a young Argentine who departed suddenly last Autumn after some sort of scandal (she will only say 'under a cloud').

The man at the lab tells us that the spool has been exposed. But my question to you is this: How long does film 'keep' in the refrigerator? This one has a date written on it which shows that it was taken twenty years ago. Do you think it likely that the pictures are still there? And if so, should one take special precautions with the developing? I hope you are not offended by my writing on such a mundane matter after so long an interval. You of all people will understand, I think, that we are intrigued to discover what is on the negatives and anxious not to spoil them. If they prove to be of interest, I would be happy to share them with you. What do you think?

With my heart-felt thanks (very much in advance!) and warm wishes,

Your old associate,

[Signed] Karl-Heinz

Letter 4

D. Skinner to Gomes, c.*1980, Amherst (orig. in English)*

Gomes –

You are mistaken to suppose that I am one iota concerned about your 'research'. My supervisor received your grubby little parcel of 'proof' and passed it on to me. I am returning it to you with my compliments. Shout it from the rooftops, if you will, and let's see whose good name is blackened. Do not bother me or my colleagues again. If you make any attempt to contact me, I will not hesitate to go to the Authorities, who know more about this matter and your part in it than you think.

D. Skinner

Letter 5

Jimmy (James P.) to José, 1980, Queens (orig. in English)

March 12th 80

My dear José –

Received this morning yours of the 8th from La Rochelle which is near Johannesburg I guess. These few lines may give you an idea of how time flew by and answer some of the questions you bombarded me with. Once more I repeat there was nothing untoward about the change in name. Try to see it as it is Brother. This is a new country where many people come to seize their opportunities. You see your world as it is, but remember that you and I have been moving in two different spheres. When long ago I attempted to get 'nat. papers' it was better to be 'James' than to be 'Tiago' of old. Remember that it was many years ago and the world was a different place. As it is I never did need any such paper since, whether to collect post or get a license or vote. When it comes to mind-their-own-business I am glad I reside in the US of A. As to the 'P' it is also a let us say 'Brain-wave'. There are so many Jimmies here hence the P. It was also a sentimental tie to the time Uncle Pedro ('Peter') came to visit and Mother appointed me guardian over the same. I took a shine to the guy. We sat on a bench at the river eating wallnuts and bread looking at the ducks?! Hardly speaking!! Benvenuti is a semi-private rooming-house. The owners are from Trinidade and the boarders live up and over the first floor. That is my haunt but I am actually across the Expressway at the actual house, small as it is, with a place to myself in the basement. Underground! I have known them for quite a while and we get along. There are many people from the islands and more everyday. I dare say if I arrived in S. Ozone Park today I would still be Tiago and no problem and you would not say I must be embarrased about the family than which nothing is further from the Truth. I was sure pleased with the pictures you sent and to hear about Óbidos. I can still see the bougainvilia where Mother used to knit and exchange confidences (Mrs Rocha). Poor Óbidos. Mother and Father's picture was wonderful but Oh boy it hurts. I have to mention being advised by the Bank of another 'donation'. Are you sure you have enough for yourself. La Rochelle sounds grand but perhaps Johannesburg is not as dear as all that. I was worried for a while over your health in those parts! You should get you a set of teeth. I have a few left and some to pull. But you will be around for sometime yet! Pick a good place to eat and watch the girls go by. We have grill houses and ice cream parlors here to beat the band. The best Sundae is the 'Screwball's Delight' but I like (you can imagine why) the one called a 'Joe Sent Me'. Just thanks again for all you have done for me. Cheer up. The BEST is yet to come.

Mar 16th The weather has kept me from the PO. You must by now have my last letter and picture. You will see that in spite of 'James' there is a Brotherly resemblance.

I have held this letter for ever so long. Today is April 1st but no fooling! Received this morning your p.c. from Durban. You are restless as always! Are you away from 'Joe-burg' often? Make sure you get my last letter addressed to 'La Rochelle' it holds a v. precious picture which I am sure you will enjoy. Some of my letters did come back in the past. Keep looking for a wealthy widow with a nice house. We are still in Winter here. It is dragging on infinitely. Yours, Jimmy (alias James P.)!

The Reading

Her reading voice was a soft-grained monotone that sifted through the open minds of the audience like sand from a clenched fist. They were practised listeners, mostly, lovers of literature and keen observers of political developments in the South, two hundred and fourteen of them according to the receipts at the door, gathered together in the Literaturhaus to hear the sorrowful story of Maryam Akello's life. She read in her native Acholi, and except for her guardian, who sat in the middle of the front row, no one in the room understood a word. They could no longer recall if they had ever heard the language spoken in a seminar or on some documentary soundtrack. They were therefore in no position to judge whether she was reading badly or well, nor to ascertain which passages of *Sugar* she had chosen to present, and this knowledge would have to wait until the second part of the programme, when her translator would read the same passages from the German version just published by Kleinbach.

That was the translator Hans Günther Basch on the podium, with his chair pushed back from the table and angled ever so slightly towards the lectern where she stood reading, his faceted crew cut tilted deferentially, deflecting the audience's attention to her and capturing a modest portion of it for himself. Although he appeared to be listening, Basch's thoughts were elsewhere. The fact is he too understood no Acholi. In preparing his German version, he had relied on the English and French editions already published and the commentary of a friend at the Goethe University in Frankfurt, an East Africa specialist. Akello herself spoke English well and they had discussed his translation in depth. He felt he knew his way around in her world. Now, as a dusty cloud of Acholi rose before his window on Africa, obscuring the landscape of the text, his thoughts returned to the introductory talk given by Prof. Horst Grundmann, another friend in the academic world, a fellow Africanist. There he was in the front row of the audience next to the writer's guardian, with his long legs stretched out, his bearded chin on his chest, the shiny top of his head aglow.

The two of them had served together for several years now on the board of the Literaturhaus. This evening's reading was an important one, the first in a series by Writers under Fire, as they called it, writers threatened or restricted or silenced by oppressive states, or driven from their countries by conflict or persecution, like Maryam Akello. It had taken a great deal of time and effort to raise the money and win the backing of the city and the sponsors, and so this inaugural event was crucial. All in all, Horst had made a good job of the introduction, Hans Günther thought, he had spoken passionately about the need, in our post-9/11 world, to celebrate difference and support dialogue, to create networks of understanding and solidarity, reminding the audience of the many countries where, even now, writers were afraid to put their own names on their texts, let alone read from them in public, and choosing your words was still a matter of life and death. Basch, who had thought himself inured to such appeals, was stirred. Yes, he had to hand it to Horst, he had done a good job of it. It was a speech calculated to assure the funders that they had spent their money wisely and the audience that they had taken a small but meaningful stand against tyranny.

With the exception of a young man towards the back of the room, who had come here with a new girlfriend to demonstrate the sincerity of his interest in her interests, every member of the audience had been to a literary reading before. A majority had been to a dozen readings or more, and a handful to hundreds. Among them, they had seen and heard thousands of writers read from their work. By the time Maryam Akello reached the bottom of the first page and peeled it over on the lectern, and while the less experienced listeners were still absorbing her tones and gestures, examining her clothes, her face and the complicated weave of her hairstyle, the old hands had already found a place for her on the shelf.

In general, they found writers easier to classify than their books. For all the variation, from the studied sing-song of American poets and booming declamations of African praise singers to the weather-report burble of certain English novelists, they fell into two broad classes: those who were at ease on the stage and those who were not. Those who gestured and projected and gave their characters accents and mannerisms, and those who simply read in their own voices, as well as they could, until it was over. The performers and the rest. Yet it was not obvious who the crowd-pleasers would be. Melodrama was always an ill-judged grimace away and some of the whisperers and mumblers made you sit up and listen.

Prompted by Akello's floury monotone, Prof. Steffi Ziegler was dwelling on these things. The professor, who lectured in twentieth-century American theatre at the University of Cologne, found herself thinking about Edward Sheldon, an all-but-forgotten playwright. She had been browsing lately through Eric Barnes's biography of Sheldon, *The Man Who Lived Twice*, and a wisp of the story was still drifting in her mind.

Like many lives touched by catastrophe, Sheldon's fell open into two unequal chapters. In the first decade of the twentieth century, he had established himself, precociously, as one of the stars of the American theatre. His play *Romance* became the stage sensation of the war years, running for season after season on Broadway, touring everywhere, going on to record-breaking runs in London and Paris. But when he was still in his twenties, he was struck down by a virulent form of arthritis, which rendered him immobile. By 1925 he was bedridden; by 1930 he was blind.

Sheldon spent the last twenty years of his life flat on his back in his Manhattan penthouse, unable to move a limb. Yet the remarkable thing is that he remained at the centre of the theatre world. Despite the severity of his affliction, he sustained friendships with hundreds of people, guiding marriages and careers, offering advice on life and work, amusing and inspiring everyone he knew. His generous, resilient spirit moved one friend to remark, 'It would have been an impertinence to pity him.'

Prof. Ziegler had written several papers on Sheldon's troublesome plays, notably *The Nigger* and *The Princess Zim-Zim*, troublesome because, despite their audacity and charm, they were disfigured by the prejudices of his time. But these concerns belonged in her scholarly work. She was musing now on the question of reading aloud. After he went blind, one of Sheldon's main pastimes was being read to. He slept little and fitfully, and every waking moment, night or day, when he was not receiving a visitor, was passed reading. Even his night nurses had to be accomplished readers and he had very specific requirements in this regard. He did not enjoy expressive reading at all. He favoured a blank monotone that allowed him to apply his own emphases, like tints on a black-and-white photograph, 'as though he were receiving the words directly from the printed page', as his biographer puts it. This he called the 'sewing machine' style of reading, a precise, regular tacking along the lines of type, seaming one imagination to another.

Maryam Akello was that kind of reader, Prof. Ziegler thought. But without knowledge of the language, it was impossible to add a single bright thread of your own to her white linen. In fact –

and at this thought Prof. Ziegler made a small, surprised sound that irritated the woman next to her – you could not even be sure it was linen. Or white.

Akello came to the end of another page – her book had yet to be published in Acholi and she was reading from a typescript – turned it over and flowed on. Shutting her eyes, Prof. Ziegler concentrated on the stream of sound. She could almost feel the little beads of it striking her eyelids. Not a sewing machine, she decided, but a more robust contraption, a planter perhaps, scattering seeds onto the harrowed earth.

By now, many of the listeners had decided that Maryam Akello was not a good reader, but their attention did not waver. Listening, like reading aloud, is an art. The silence was more than polite: it expressed the general feeling of the audience that *Sugar* was a good book. This was largely thanks to Horst Grundmann, whose article some of them had read in *Die Zeit* the week before, publicising the reading and the series it inaugurated. All of them, with the exception of a student who had arrived late and was leaning against the wall at the back beside the TV camera, had also just heard Prof. Grundmann's introductory speech and so they had some idea what the reading might be about even if they did not understand. Having first set out the aims of the Writers under Fire initiative, and thanked the partner organisations and sponsors in the city government and the private sector, he had gone on to tell how Akello and her sister had been abducted from a village in northern Uganda by the Lord's Resistance Army and carried off into slavery in Sudan. After much suffering, she had miraculously escaped and ended up in the refugee camp at Koboko, only for this place of apparent refuge to come under attack by rebels. Once again, she was lucky to escape with her life. With the help of Christian missionaries, she had reached the United States, which she now regarded as her home. *Sugar*, published there with the support of UNESCO, had been an unexpected success. It was unusual, Prof. Grundmann said, for such a dark story to become a bestseller, but no one who read it could fail to be moved by the spirit of the writer, which was bathed in light. The German translation by Hans Günther Basch, one of the finest practitioners in the field, was the fourth foreign-language edition, and half a dozen more were on the cards.

Throughout Grundmann's speech, Akello had sat immobile. She understood no German, and there was no simultaneous translation this evening, but she had a notion of what her host was saying because he had thoughtfully sent her the gist of his speech in an email. Although her face appeared open and frank, it was turned slightly to one side and her gaze was averted, as if she were watching something in the corner of her eye. It seemed to several people on the opposite side of the auditorium, including a young poet in the fourth row from the front, that her heavy-lidded eyes were actually closed.

Behind the lectern she appeared to be even smaller than she was, scarcely more than a girl. When she reached for the microphone it shrieked and she pulled away as if a placid dog had snapped at her. A technician, crouching so that he would not obscure the view of the audience or the cameraman even for a moment, slipped in from one side, expertly adjusted the stand to bring the mic close to her mouth, and slipped away.

Prof. Ziegler, who had spoken briefly to Akello in the lobby fifteen minutes earlier, and twenty other members of the audience who had heard her being interviewed on the radio the day before, expected her to say a few words in English. In fact, she had intended to read from the English translation. But when they'd met in the café of the Literaturhaus to discuss the order of proceedings, Prof. Grundmann proposed that she read in Acholi instead and Hans Günther supported him. It was an opportunity for her to use her own language, they said, to speak in her own voice. It was important for the audience too, hearing the cadences of the original would open their minds to another world. She would be free to speak English afterwards, of course, when she took questions from the floor. Nearly everyone in Germany spoke English. So now, once the microphone had been adjusted, she simply tapped her typescript on the top of the lectern, producing two discreet hammer blows that called the gathering to order, set the pages down and began to read.

In the moment when the sheaf of papers was visible above the lectern, seven people in the audience assessed how thick it was and thus how long the reading might last. Yet the calculation was not a sign of impatience or boredom on their part, nor was there any indication of this on the part of anyone else. The room was silent and attentive. It was, thought Annemieke Vogel, who was reporting on the event for the *Süddeutsche Zeitung*, unusually silent for such a large crowd. Perhaps it was the effect of this slight woman and her whispery voice. Someone coughed quietly into a fist, a chair squeaked, and the audience seemed to suck in its belly and lean closer.

That soft, synthetic squeak ran like a skewer through Karolina Fischer, the events coordinator of the Literaturhaus. She remembered again a board meeting at which she had argued, in vain, that plastic seat covers were impractical (she could not say vulgar). But no one had taken her seriously. She had been made to feel petty, glances were exchanged, there she goes again. She'd had a point though. Usually it was not too bad in a crowd this size, which shuffled, rustled, coughed and scratched sufficiently to drown out the childishly obscene noises of the cushions, but in smaller gatherings it was embarrassing. Especially if the book was a serious one and there were no opportunities for laughter to break the tension. She would raise the matter at the next meeting. The chairs were three years old, they could replace or reupholster them now without appearing wasteful.

Intent though he appeared to be on the reading, as befitted a translator, Hans Günther Basch was studying the footwear of his friend Horst Grundmann, which the angle of his head had placed in his line of vision. Leather hiking boots with rubber soles. The man was a famous walker, always tramping through a forest or over a hill, restless and indefatigable. He would come back from a hike flushed and triumphant, with moss smeared on the seat of his pants and hillocks of snow on his toecaps, and tramp mud up and down the corridors of the Department to show that he had been abroad, that he was not some desk-bound egghead afraid of the outdoors. There was something embedded there in the treads of his boots, a brand name probably, in an oval frame. It really did look like a brand, like a sign you would burn into the hide of a cow. It was a sole that would make a deep impression in a flower bed beneath the window of a vicarage. Basch didn't have the stomach for the hard-boiled private eyes the publishers were always pressing on him, but he liked the old-fashioned ones like Hercule Poirot and Father Brown. As he watched Grundmann's boots swivelling on their heels – big feet, perhaps a 48, he thought – he wondered how often a footprint helped to catch a thief or a murderer. Did they really fill them with plaster of Paris and present them in court? There was probably some synthetic modern substitute, like resin or silicone. These days everything was a gel. Footprint, one said, although strictly it was a shoeprint, a soleprint.

While he was thinking this, Hans Günther's eyes wandered to the glass wall that ran down one side of the room. There had been quite a bit of argument about that between the board and the architect. It would make the space cold, they said, especially in the winter. But the architect had argued that a place like the Literaturhaus needed to be open to the world, it was part of the symbolic logic of the building, and she was right, people often passed by outside during a reading and that sense of life going on, of the city outside, made the words on the page seem more vital. Not that there was anyone out there now: just the cold square covered in snow and the avenue of beeches with their skinny trunks and naked limbs.

Some familiar word, a husk of sense in the granular outflow of Maryam Akello's reading, snagged Basch's attention and he became aware of her voice again. What was that word? It sounded like magic or make-believe. A foodstuff. Some kind of millet? He remembered discussing it with her. She had come to see him at his apartment to iron out the problems with his translation. He'd cleared a space among the books and papers on the kitchen table, which was never used for eating at, and opened his working manuscript between them. It was stuck all over with notes and queries on yellow Post-its and they'd spent the entire morning going from one to the next. She had the Acholi typescript in a box file beside her, but she did not refer to it once. Perhaps she knew the text by heart. On the chair beside him lay the published English edition, also laden with notes in green, and the French one bristling with blue, but they did not open them either. While he raised his doubts and asked his questions, she pored over the German version as if she understood it, and he made notes and revisions on the manuscript with a pencil or a fountain pen, her English explanations and his German equivalents, often shadowed by question marks. The discarded Post-its, covered with deletions and options, heaped up in an ashtray at the corner of the table.

He invited her to stay for lunch, but her guardian was waiting for her at the hotel. They had to meet a photographer from *Der Spiegel*, and then they were leaving that very evening for Osnabrück, where she was doing a reading at the Felix Nussbaum Museum tomorrow, and so he walked her to the station at the end of the block and made sure she got on the right tram.

They parted cheerfully, anticipating a reunion soon enough when the book was published, but as he walked back home a dark mood settled over him. His legs and his heart grew heavy.

He had held this feeling at bay all through the long months of work on the translation, forcing himself to keep his professional distance and focus on the job at hand. Meeting her in person, sitting with her at his kitchen table with their knees practically touching, had closed the space between them. It was unspeakable, what had happened to her; it could scarcely be imagined. Yet she had made something of it, she had written it down, without a trace of self-pity. He climbed the stairs to his apartment, and everything made him sad: the bicycles with their training wheels on the landings, the rubber overshoes in three sizes at the front door of the downstairs neighbour, like an illustration from *The Story of the Three Bears*, the sheen of the wooden balustrade under his hand, the glimpses of rooftops and chimneys through the windows. When he shut his front door behind him there were tears in his eyes, but he swallowed the sob pushing up in his throat. He could not weep when she herself was so composed. It would be an insult. Was it strength, this self-possession of hers? Or had something been undone in her, permanently disconnected, short-circuited? She gave away so little. It was as if she had told the story and kept it to herself at the same time. As if she had concealed it precisely by sharing it.

It's a waltz, thought the young woman who had arrived late, as Akello came to the end of another page, peeled it over and went on. One two three, one two three.

Four of the page-counters estimated that Akello had reached the halfway mark and that she was now on the downhill slope.

Prof. Ziegler got an itch under her thigh but could not scratch it without annoying the woman beside her, who had already given her several cautionary glances. She was reminded again of poor Edward Sheldon, lying immobile on his catafalque in his Upper East Side apartment, unable to move a finger. He was lucky to have a squad of minders to minister to his needs, she thought, to have night nurses and cooks, and the money to pay them. But the word 'lucky' troubled her in relation to someone so direly afflicted. How frustrated he must have been. And then she wondered how he had passed water and whether he had bodily urges and what he did about them.

The young man who had come with his girlfriend read the blurb on the back of the book, which he was holding for her; she wanted to get it signed afterwards. He wondered what life was like in Uganda now and whether there were wildlife reserves there.

Florence Lawino, the author's guardian, the only person in the room who heard Akello's voice falter as she began to tell about the murder of her sister, slipped her hand through the gap between two buttons on her blouse and touched the scar on her own stomach.

Something else came back to Hans Günther. It was later on the day of her visit, when he was clearing up the kitchen table, that he came across the ashtray full of Post-its. It was like a little bonfire and he felt like putting a match to it. But that was absurd. He stripped off the first of the notes and looked at it. 'Resurrected?' it read in his blue pen. And then in pencil the word she had suggested: 'translated'. And then in blue again: 'brought back, raised, revived?' He always had other ideas. That was the problem with translation: there was always another possibility. Which made her suggestion doubly difficult. Why had she said 'translated'? *Translated from the dead.* As if death itself were a language, the source language, and translation a matter of faith. Suddenly the whole enterprise felt hopeless. He opened the English version and read the phrase to himself again: *brought back from the dead.* It made more sense. Then he picked up the French version but did not open it. It had one of those unfussy French covers of clean white board upon which floated a picture the size of a playing card; a cross section of sugar cane in close-up, cut off between the earth and the sky. He gazed at it in despair.

It would have intrigued Hans Günther Basch to learn that

Florence Lawino, whose hand caught his attention as it stirred beneath the fabric of her blouse, had a life story every bit as harrowing as her charge's. But she had never spoken about it outside the counselling room, let alone written it down. The two of them had journeyed independently to America, but they had been placed in the same foster home because their stories were so alike. They discovered that they had grown up in villages not far apart in the Gulu District. Florence too had been abducted, she had even been in Koboko a few months before Maryam, but had left before the rebel attack. She was a little younger than Maryam, but she had become her guardian nevertheless.

She had heard Maryam speak or read at scores of briefings, conferences and workshops. In the beginning, the telling of the story, which was so like her own, left her feeling exposed, sometimes angry, but she got used to it and these days it hardly bothered her. She thought every day about what had happened to her and these memories were more vivid than any scene that could be conjured up in words by someone else. In any event, it was different here, on this evening, with Maryam reading in Acholi while the trees stood aghast behind the glass with their feet in the snow. It was as if Maryam was speaking only to her.

As she listened to the story, so familiar she could recite parts of it by heart, her hand moved along the livid blanket stitch of scar tissue. With her middle finger she followed the ridge from her navel to her hipbone, tracing each of the eleven stitches, first the part above the slash and then the part below, while in her mind she passed down a corridor, trying the doors on one side and then the other, and found them all locked.

There were no clues in Akello's reading to indicate when she might stop: the listeners could not judge whether a passage was rising to a climax or falling to a resolution, and so their attention was not modulated by the usual sense of anticipation that accompanies a reading in a familiar language. She gave nothing away, neither speeding up nor slowing down, and never once looking up from the page. Again Andrij Leonenko, the young poet in the fourth row, had the impression that her eyes were closed and she was reciting from memory. She turned the pages so precisely, rolling back one after the other with exactly the same gesture and without licking her finger. When she did stop it was not abrupt but final, given the same flat emphasis with which she had begun. She did not smile or say thank you. She gathered up her papers, squared them once against the lectern and went back to her seat.

The audience drifted for a moment on the receding tide of her voice, then roused themselves and applauded. At the same time, they began to do all the things people do when the hold of a crowd relaxes and releases them back into their separate bodies, sitting up straight, stretching their legs, arching their backs, craning their necks, clearing their throats.

To Karolina Fischer, the events coordinator of the Literaturhaus, the squealing and screeching from the chairs was intolerable. It was like the cacophony that arose when you walked into the House of Tropical Birds at the Tiergarten. But before she could start going over the whole saga of the chairs in her mind, something distracted her. She noticed that the woman next to her was wearing some kind of safari suit, and that the khaki tunic had tiny patches of leopard skin scattered over it at random, triangles and parallelograms with loose flaps and tabs that suggested they had a purpose that was not simply decorative, like storing bullets or securing a water bottle or a bush knife.

As the applause drained away, the members of the audience began to do many other things with their hands, patting their knees, straightening their skirts, winding off scarves, pushing back cuffs to glance at watches, folding the creased and sweaty programmes they had been holding and putting them in their handbags, retrieving the crisp progammes they had put away in their handbags and smoothing them out on their laps, fumbling in the pockets of the jackets hanging over the backs of their chairs for tissues, cough lozenges, antacid tablets, lip balm, cleaning their glasses on the tails of their shirts, rubbing their palms together, covering their yawning mouths. Nearly all of those who were on their own checked their cellphones for messages; nearly all of those who had company turned to their companions to exchange stored-up observations.

The young man who was attending his first literary reading said that it was fascinating, he was enjoying himself very much, but the way he said it made his new girlfriend wonder whether he was telling the truth, and anyway how could you enjoy something that was so sad, even if you couldn't follow the exact words?

Prof. Ziegler scratched the inside of her thigh, although it was not really itchy any more, and then turning to survey the room behind her caught the eye of an old student of hers a few rows back. He mouthed an enquiry after her health and she smiled and nodded and mouthed that she was fine, fine.

Andrij Leonenko took out a small red notebook with a spiral binding, turned to a clean page and, shielding it from view with his free hand, jotted down a phrase that had come to him ten minutes earlier and might be the first line of a poem: 'You read with your eyes closed.'

Horst Grundmann leant over to his wife Sylvia and asked her whether she had remembered to let Bertram know about Thursday, and she said yes, he'd said it was no problem. And then he leant to the other side and said to Florence that Maryam had read superbly, and Florence said yes, it had been very good.

Rolf Backer, the commissioning editor from Kleinbach, a tall man who usually covered his shaven head with a soft felt hat that made him feel (and he hoped look) like a writer himself, but which he had checked at the cloakroom out of consideration for the people sitting behind him, remarked to his companion Theo van Roosbroeck, a Belgian political theorist who had written about the militia in the Democratic Republic of Congo, that Akello was a brave girl, and Theo replied that she was pretty too, although she'd had the stuffing knocked out of her, understandably so, and they agreed that it was a terrible thing that had happened to her, but that she'd overcome adversity in a way that was truly inspiring. To himself, Theo noted that people in Europe were tired of stories like this, sad as they were, and wondered whether his friend Rolf might not find it easier to market someone who gave the impression of being less resigned to her fate.

Three people who had other arrangements for the evening and one who'd decided he'd had enough listening for one day slipped out of their rows, excuse me, thank you, and headed for the exits. Two people immediately put something – a coat, a spindled programme – on the empty seats to discourage someone else from sitting there. The student who had been leaning against the wall at the back quickly took the nearest vacated seat with nothing on it, noted that the shiny plastic still retained the imprint of the departed backside, and for that reason did not like the residual warmth she felt through the fabric of her skirt.

The poet Leonenko took out his notebook for the second time and wrote 'Reader, open your eyes' and after that a question mark in a circle, like a copyright notice. Earlier that week, his very first poem had been accepted for publication in *Die Horen* and his editor there had told him not to be scared to write things down. Every poem started with a single word.

Meanwhile Hans Günther Basch passed behind Maryam Akello, who had taken her seat again at the table. He reached out to squeeze her shoulder, in passing, but thought better of it at the last moment and instead squeezed the cushion of her chair. He put his copy of *Zucker* down on the lectern with the passages he intended to read flagged in yellow. He raised the microphone stand, and then dropped it and raised it again, as if he were measuring the difference in their heights, and then he puffed into the mesh bauble once. He took off his glasses and put them in the breast pocket of his jacket. His reading glasses with their pointy Brechtian frames were already hanging around his neck on a chain. He waited for the room to settle.

Without his glasses, the room looked shapeless and steamy. He thought he saw Horst and Sylvia with their heads together, and then Maryam in the front row. No, of course, it couldn't be Maryam who was on the podium, it was Anya. No, no, not Anya, what was he thinking? Anya was in the book, she was dead, or rather translated from the dead. It was Florence.

Of the one hundred and forty-five people who happened to be watching Hans Günther then, eleven noticed the momentary bewilderment that crossed his face as he glanced at Maryam Akello and then at the audience, tucking in his chin as if he were afraid of being hit, and they put it down to nerves or irritation at how long the room was taking to come to order.

He remembered sitting at his kitchen table a few days after Maryam's visit, with the manuscript open beside his laptop, inputting the revisions they had discussed. He was working through the grimmest passage in the book – it was among those he was about to read – where she described the murder of her sister. This had to be perfect. Even after every second word had been changed and changed again, he wondered whether the tone was right, whether he had captured the original, whether the depths of feeling in it had found some resonance in his own language. As he turned to a new page of the manuscript, he saw a note in red ink. No one but Maryam had touched these pages: she must have written it while he was out of the room. He looked closer. She had added a line in the last paragraph about the sugar. There were his questions in pencil: Is this really what you want to say? Did your English translator understand properly? Is there not a softer phrase? There was the note in blue ink he had written to himself in German at the end of the discussion, when she appeared to agree with him that some things were better left unsaid. And then there was this new line, her final word on the subject, written in blood in the narrow margin. A judgement.

An expectant hush drew him back into the present. For a moment the silent room felt like a clearing in the forest, cloven in two by the shimmering stream of the aisle. He became aware of the heads of the audience like moss-covered rocks, and the thoughts condensed above them like mist in the early morning, and then the trees beyond the window, receding into the dark. With both hands, he lifted the dangling glasses from his chest, placed them squarely before his eyes, and began.

I am in the middle now. In the beginning, when we walked, the ropes that keep us joined together pulled tight and every few paces one of us nearly fell or dropped the box or bundle she was carrying. In the beginning? It was only yesterday. Today we are moving like a creature with a supple spine and many arms and legs. They said we would soon learn to cooperate and we have. The reason is simple: they will kill us if we don't. Drop the sorghum, the bullets, the radio and you will be cut loose like a vine. They will not waste a shot on you. We have learnt to keep so close together that there is slack in the ropes even when we clamber over rocks or slide down cuttings.

Yesterday, Anya was behind me. But last night they split us into two groups and this morning they tied us differently. Now she is right in front and I am in the middle. Between the two of us, the girl called Amito and a boy who never speaks and does not yet have a name. Behind me, our neighbour from Atiak, and then her niece, and then the other boy, the one who called out to Amito when the Commander took her away to the fire last night. I think he may be her brother and his name is Kidega.

Perhaps I could learn to tell us apart by the different sounds we make. Amito's skirt is full and starchy and it makes a different sound to my own, which has been worn soft by washing. The Atiak neighbour swallows the air with a rasp as if its edges are sharp. I also hear the pad of our soles on the path and the creaking of the boxes and bags we carry on our heads, like the sound a cow makes as it moves. Under it all, my heart beating, setting the pace. It would be pleasant, almost a kind of walking music, if things were different, if we were somewhere else and not here with these men.

They make a noise of their own. I hear their heels striking the ground, the clinking of buckles, the stock of a rifle tapping against a button, water sloshing in bottles. If we are an animal, they are a machine, some heavy weapon we have to drag along.

There are seven of them too, one for each of us, although that is the wrong way to put it because it is no more than a coincidence. One of them could subdue us. They have guns and boots and we do not even have shoes. They are men and we are children. Anya is the eldest, I think, and she is not even eighteen yet. Perhaps they planned to capture more of us? That would explain why they are so angry. If we were twice as many, they could kill a few of us to teach the others a lesson. But now they have to take care of us or the whole business will be for nothing.

I can hardly tell which one is which. They keep changing places and they look the same in their uniforms and berets. One of them has a beard, and one has sunglasses with pink frames, and one of them is the Commander. Also I cannot look too hard, because when Kidega, the boy who may be Amito's brother, looked at the Commander this morning, he hit him in the face and told him to keep his eyes on the Lord.

Mostly, I watch Anya, to give myself courage. I am glad she is in front of me. Once, when the path turned sharply, she looked at me just for a moment. It was the kind of look she would give me when Father was angry about something silly and there was no point in arguing with him. That one look was like a whole conversation. Since then, I have been watching the curve of her shoulder, the muscle in her arm raised to steady the box, the way her calves flex as she walks, and I know she is telling me something. Be strong.

Hans Günther Basch took a deep breath and put his thumb on the yellow Post-it that marked the second passage he meant to read. The audience's attention had been drifting between the reader and the writer, settling now on Basch, telling the story, now on Akello, who had lived it and was perhaps reliving it, although her expression remained remote, which made it difficult for them to picture her in the role. The sticky note got caught on Basch's forefinger and he lost his place. There was a silence, given texture by some scuffing and coughing, while he leafed through the book in search of the passage he had marked. Just a brief section, but important, if one was to convey the story. The attention converged on him and cohered. In the instant before it fell apart, he found the pencilled bracket at the start of the paragraph and went on.

When I awake, the bearded one is standing over me, with his boots pressed to my thighs, pinning me to the ground by the cloth of my skirt. He blots out the firelight, the branches of the trees grow out of his body like thorny, crooked arms. Then the sky falls on me and I am choking on the bristle-brush hairs of his chest and the fabric of his shirt, which smells of smoke and sweat. The earth swallows me. Just as I am sinking into the darkness, he rises up and my hips lift off the ground, and then his head burrows into my belly and rolls from side to side, as if he is wiping his mouth on me. He blows out hot breath and spit, and then he pulls away again and drops me on the ground. Without a word, he goes to Anya, unthreads her from the rest of us like a bead from a string and takes her away. She doesn't make a sound.

. . .

Another line had come into Leonenko's head, the line 'Reader, close your eyes', and he thought of writing it down in the red notebook, but the fact that Hans Günther Basch was looking straight at him, or so it seemed, made it impossible.

Horst Grundmann thought his friend Hans Günther looked a little feverish and wondered whether he was coming down with something, or whether perhaps he'd been hitting the bottle; he used to have that problem, although everyone thought he was on the wagon these days.

The young man who was attending his first reading wondered if there was surfing in Zanzibar. He had seen something about snorkelling there on television, but he had always wanted to learn to surf. Perhaps he would ask her during question time. She was from that part of the world.

Prof. Ziegler remembered that the former student who was sitting a few rows behind her had written a very interesting thesis on the use of the mask in Greek tragedy in relation to self-dramatisation and the stylisation of emotion in the contemporary media, and she thought she should collar him afterwards and ask if he had finished that article based on his research. They had one slot to fill in the Spring edition of *Exeunt*.

Rolf Backer, the editor at Kleinbach, remembered the annual sales conference which was coming up and the spreadsheets on his computer at the office with their breakdowns of typesetting costs, marketing plans, review copies and sales projections, and the report from the distribution agency about book shops closing down, even in Leipzig, and how the ebook was the way to go, and he put his head in his hands and began to massage his scalp.

The student who had come in late and had to stand for the first half of the reading, but who was now sitting directly behind Rolf Backer, stared at his fingers as they prodded the rubbery pink skin of his scalp, which he had shaved that morning, the fingertips sunk in the flesh and shifting it around on the bone, forcing it into ridges and ripples, stretching out the long, furrowed crease that ran down into the collar of his jacket, and she could not look away even though the sight of it made her queasy.

There were no flies on Maryam Akello, Rolf was thinking. She'd had the sense to go to live in America. All the good African writers were in America or England. It was a big plus on the marketing side.

Hans Günther ran his eye down the passage he was about to read. How to speak these words? This was the inspiring part; it was painful but uplifting. It had given the book its title and had already been extracted in one of the papers. A few people in the audience were sure to be familiar with it. He must do it justice.

I keep the days in my pocket. Each day is a stone and so far there are only three of them, Wednesday, Thursday and Friday. It is easy to hold three days in your head, but it will not be easy in a week or a month.

The Commander has warned us not to complain about walking or carrying. Get used to it, he says, you will be doing it for a long time. If you cannot go on, you will be killed. The choice is yours.

He also says: You have come too far to find your way home. Which way will you go? What will you eat? Think how much harder it will be in two weeks' time. Then it will be impossible to run away. We won't even bother to tie you.

I turn the stones over and press one against the palm of my hand with my little finger. This hollow one is Thursday. Yesterday.

Yesterday I was glad that Anya was walking in front of me. I felt that she was showing me the way. Today I wish she was behind me, so I did not have to see the blood and ash on the back of her dress. She is like a smudged drawing. I hardly recognise the lines of her body.

Today, Friday, is a round pebble, perfectly smooth except for a thin, rough seam around its middle. When I picked it up I saw that it was dark, almost black, with a yellowish vein running through it like fat in a piece of meat.

I keep the days in one pocket. I keep the sugar in the other.

This morning, something glistened on my wrist and when I passed it over my lips I tasted sugar. Reaching to the top of the bag on my head, I pushed my finger into the fold and found that it has pulled open there. The gap is just wide enough for the tip of a thumb and forefinger. A pinch of sweetness.

It is our sugar. It belongs to my family. The soldiers took it from our larder when they took us. Just as they took the sack of sorghum that Amito is carrying from her mother's kitchen. It gives me a purpose here. I am watching over our things.

Mother was always so careful with the sugar. Waste not, want not. You had to be sure not to spill a single grain opening a new bag. Some sugar might be caught in the folds of the paper.

I steady the bag with one hand, reach into the opening and pinch a few grains between my fingers. After a few paces I raise the sugar to my lips. Sweetness. And sweat.

We are in the open now, following a path along the grassy ridge of a hill. It was a relief to come out from under the trees. It is hotter here but the path is open and that makes the carrying easier. I worry about Anya. She has stumbled a few times even though the path is good. She is carrying the box with the bullets, the heaviest thing even though it is made of plastic, even heavier than the radio. They gave it to her because she is the tallest. I watch her back but it says nothing. Perhaps the sugar feels lighter because it is sweet? We have eaten nothing but scraps since we left Atiak. When we pass a mango tree they will not let us pick the fruit.

I am taking sugar for this evening. I had the idea to hide some in my pocket as we walk, so that tonight when we are tied up together I can share it with Anya. I must be careful not to let them see what I am doing or to tear the opening in the bag. If they think I have stolen from them, they will kill me. Even though the sugar is actually mine.

I look for a landmark on the path ahead, a dead tree or an ant-hill, and wait until we are there before I reach into the bag again.

The first pinch turns to syrup on my fingertips. I have to wipe the sweat off my palm on the hem of my skirt and try again. This time I manage to carry a pinch of sugar to my pocket, but then I can't be sure it is still there. Perhaps it fell into the stitching of the seam and my poking finger pushed it deeper or melted it to nothing. I must be patient.

We walk all morning. It is Friday, a black pebble with a vein of yellow fat in it, which no tongue will ever taste. Stone, sugar. Once Amito says that she cannot go on and sinks down under the sack, but they shout at her until she gets up again. One of the younger soldiers, he is no older than me, hits her on the shoulder with the flat side of his panga. Let me kill this one, he shouts. But the Commander says, Then who will carry this sack?

At midday, they let us drink from a stream they have muddied with their boots. They eat cold porridge from the night before, from the hollow belly of Thursday, and we get the crusts scraped from the bottom of the pot. There are stalks of grass or tobacco in mine but I swallow it just like that.

The niece of the neighbour from Atiak does not eat. She cries softly. Her heels are bleeding. She is from town and not used to walking. We are used to walking at home, but not this far, carrying such heavy things, without rest. My feet are also swollen. Anya and I kneel down together at the stream to drink and I try to show her how sorry I am but she will not meet my eye.

We go on. I feed my pocket. There is a little store of sugar there now. I stop myself from checking how much. For all I know it is only a pinch, but I imagine a spoonful or a cupful. I imagine scooping it out in a cupped hand. Tonight, when they pile the provisions together and tie us up under a tree or on the bed of a stream, I hope Anya and I are close together. Once the others are asleep, I'll whisper in her ear and tell her to lick her finger and press it into my pocket.

Hans Günther paused again and paged forward to the last of the yellow flags. Now for the Valley of Death, he thought. And then the words she had inscribed on the manuscript. He could almost feel them through the printed page: handmade things in a world of flawless signs. His throat was tight. He pursed his lips and squeezed breath into his head as if he was trying to make his ears pop. The more practised listeners could tell by his attitude that the reading was not over, but some of the others shifted experimentally in their chairs or glanced at their companions. He ran a knuckle along the stitching to press the pages flat and looked over the edge.

The path falls into the valley. Some of the men want to stop here on the edge of the abyss, others want to press on. Amito and Kidega add their voices to the chorus. They are tired, their feet are sore, they need to rest.

It is a mistake. We have been told not to speak, neither among ourselves nor to them. The bearded one is suddenly angry. He knocks Amito to the ground. The boy with the panga is there but it is the one with the sunglasses, the one they call Shaggy, who rushes forward to beat her. He has a switch and he lashes her with it, across her back, on her shoulders, on her shins, and she cries out and tries to ward off the blows with her hands.

After half a dozen blows, I start counting, and then I stop again and look away. My face is turned to Amito, because they want us to watch, that is the point, but my eyes are not. Something is flickering down there to one side, but I cannot tell if it is something small right here on the ground beside the path or something big far away in the bottom of the valley. It twists like a flame.

There is nothing we can do, of course. Even Kidega is silent all through the beating. I wish she would get up. She is weaker than I am and more complaining. If he kills her, it will be worse for me. And who will carry the sorghum?

At last, it stops. The bearded one orders us to walk again and we get to our feet and start lifting everything. Usually one or two of the men have gone ahead on the path, leading the way, but now some of them are arguing about where to stop and others are dragging Amito to her feet, and so Anya is in front. The rest of us are still heaving up sacks and untangling ropes when she starts down the steep track with the box on her head. She has hardly taken a step before she slips on the shale and falls, pulling all of us with her, scrambling to keep our footing and set down our things. She tries to hold onto the box and so it is in her hands when it comes down on the rock, and it looks as if she has dashed it there rather than dropped it. The box breaks open at the hinges and the small cardboard boxes inside spill out, and some of them burst open too and the bullets flash and tumble down like a splash of coppery water over the rocks.

The boy raises his panga, but the Commander snaps it from his hand like a twig. Then he tramples me down in the grass as he barges past. The blade goes up into the blue and comes down from high on the scalloped neck of Anya's dress and she does not even see it fall. She calls out once, and the blade rises again and falls. Again and again.

With the final blow he cuts the rope. He wipes the blade in the grass.

They gather the boxes of bullets and stuff them into their canvas bags and their buttoned pockets. They clean the loose ones in their mouths and roll them on their thighs. Everything makes them angry. They say we are weighing them down, they should kill us all, and they hit us and drag us around on the rocks, but they do not use the panga again.

When everything has been divided, they tell us to go on, over the bridge. We have to step on this thing that was Anya, each of us, as if it were a branch fallen across a stream. This is part of the lesson.

He should stop now, Hans Günther thought, this was far enough. But it would be cowardly. She had finished it, she had pushed on to the end and kept her word, and so must he.

That was the last time I touched my sister. There was hard earth beneath my feet, and then yielding flesh, once, twice, and then rock. It was the way forward. I stepped lightly and looked ahead. As I crossed over into the future, I made a promise. I said that if I lived, I would tell this story, so that she would not be forgotten. Your breath is in these words, Anya. I have translated you from the dead.

We stopped in the hollow of the valley. The men were spent and we were too tired to be afraid or to run away. They need not have bothered to tie us up. As I lay down, with the others gasping for breath all around me, I put my hand in my pocket. And I—

Hans Günther dropped his head. His glasses, which had been sliding to the end of his nose, fell to his chest and dangled on the chain. Just a few more lines and then he was done. He did not need to see them written down. They had been sounding in his head for months. He opened his mouth and what came out was a sob.

The auditorium shook as if a wind had blown down the doors and consternation churned through the rows.

Horst Grundmann leant over towards his wife Sylvia and said that Hans Günther had not been himself lately, and although in truth such a thought had not crossed his mind before this evening, now that he had said it, it seemed true.

Andrij Leonenko took out his notebook and clasped it between his knees like a missal. He should make a note of something, he knew.

Annemieke Vogel, who had been covering the readings at the Literaturhaus for three years without noting anything even slightly out of the ordinary, felt an exhilarating jolt in her chest as she realised that something strange and remarkable was happening, followed by a tremor of dread that came with the certainty it was going to be embarrassing.

I—

Hans Günther Basch gulped. A tear eased from the corner of his right eye, ran swiftly down the slope of his nose and swerved into the corner of his mouth.

There arose, like a squall on the surface of a lake, a murmur made of many parts – surprise, curiosity, sympathy, dismay, glee – emotions that encircled one another or clashed like waves, causing flurries of turbulent conversation, muttered exclamations and undertones, chasing into every corner. Underneath it all, the chairs shrieked like a chorus of demons, but only Karolina Fischer heard them.

Maryam Akello stirred. She glanced questioningly at Hans Günther Basch, but she was the one person in the room who could not see his face clearly. Then she looked towards the front row and raised a quizzical eyebrow.

Ich—

Hans Günther gulped again. Then his face began to crumble, from the top down, like an expertly imploded building. The skin around his eyes creased and the lids sagged, allowing his tears to flow freely. These tears washed away the last vestiges of order in his features and left behind a look of utter misery. His nose broadened, opening two mazy courses of wrinkles in his cheeks, which carried the tears by roundabout routes down towards his mouth and chin. His lips drew back, becoming flat and thick, as the corners of his mouth travelled back towards his ears, and then his yellow teeth appeared, threaded with saliva. The round base of his chin dimpled and elongated into an oval cushion. The skin of his neck was spanned tight across his jawbone and the tears, passing over that cliff, coursed down into the collar of his shirt.

Bloody crybaby, Prof. Ziegler said out loud. She thought of Edward Sheldon, lying on his catafalque under a brocade coverlet, naked but for a dinner jacket, complete with bow tie and buttonhole, which was actually no more than a bib covering his chest and secured at the back with laces.

Mortified, unable to watch for a moment longer, Karolina Fischer turned to the woman beside her and asked whether her safari suit came from Uganda, and the woman said no, her sister-in-law had bought it in Cape Town, and Karolina said she didn't mean to pry and the woman said not at all, the leopard skin was synthetic, and she was welcome to look at the label in the collar if she wanted to know the name of the designer.

Andrij Leonenko slipped out of his seat and headed for the free wine in the foyer.

At that moment, the girl who had come in late had the same idea.

Rolf Backer wondered what the papers would have to say about this and whether it would be good or bad for sales, and his friend Theo van Roosbroeck, who was biting his lip so as not to burst out laughing, noticed that the woman next to him had begun to record the spectacle on her cellphone.

The young man who had never been to a reading before felt the stirring of an erection beneath the copy of *Zucker* he was holding on his lap and his new girlfriend, noticing the way he shifted in his chair and gripped the book, thought that perhaps she had misjudged him and he was quite a sensitive man after all.

Hans Günther's percussive sobs rang through the loudspeakers.

The puzzlement on Maryam Akello's face had drained away, leaving a residue of cold indifference.

Hans Günther fumbled a handkerchief from his pocket, but it may as well have been a flag of surrender. He wept as if he would never stop.

Horst Grundmann rose and turned to the audience. He crossed his arms and flung them wide and crossed them again. The gesture was meant for the cameraman. Enough, it said, switch off. Look away. When this made no impression, Horst drew the flat of his hand across his throat. Cut! For God's sake. Kill it! But the camera was unmoved.

Behind Grundmann, Maryam Akello sat quietly on the podium. In the surf of bobbing heads strangers turned to one another, all speaking at once, trying to decipher what they were witnessing, testing out what might be an adequate response or, finding that none was possible, opening their programmes and sinking into the forgiving surface of the printed page. In all this to-do, Maryam Akello sought out Florence Lawino. The look they exchanged was worth preserving for the record, but the cameraman was focused on Hans Günther Basch, stooped over the lectern with the broken pieces of his face in his hands.

The Trunks – A Complete History

Claude and his trunks. Where do I start?

Margery first told me about Claude thirty years ago. Then he was living in a flat in Braamfontein, and she would visit him there or join him for dinner from time to time. He'd been a teacher at the university once but he was no longer working. From what I could gather – and there was never much to go on, the story was full of silences – he was an antisocial and even paranoid person, but also erudite and crankily entertaining when he chose to be. In the mid-1990s, Claude, by then sickly and reclusive, came to live with Margery in Somerset Road. And it was then that she told me about the trunks. I learnt that when Claude and his father Bertrand, whom everyone knew as Berti, had arrived in Cape Town from Europe after the war, the trunks containing their possessions had been put in storage. And there they had stayed for nearly half a century. There was always some reason why it was better to leave them where they were. When Margery took Claude under her wing in Kensington, the baggage was finally retrieved. Berti was long dead by then and Claude, as it turned out, had only a few years to live.

She showed me the trunks, recently arrived by rail from the Cape and stored in the basement of her house. There were four of them: an enormous travelling chest of weathered, canvas-covered board, with hardwood slats and metal catches, so corroded they could hardly be opened; two smaller metal trunks, also rusted and dented; and an even smaller wooden chest with leather trim. Besides these, a few carpet bags, hatboxes, cardboard cartons. I looked at these things from the doorway. They were intriguing, like objects lifted from the bottom of the ocean; and they were also ominous, as if their long quarantine had failed to detoxify them or, like treasure pilfered from a grave, they might exhale some curse. They looked pale, unused to the light. The largest one was the size of a coffin and smelt of damp soil.

Occasionally, in the early years, I had been eager to meet Claude, not merely to satisfy my curiosity, but to fill in a gap in my friendship with Margery. Her mysterious friend was alive only in her accounts of him. In fact, he was so vividly present there, and so insubstantial otherwise, that I sometimes doubted whether he existed at all. But oddly enough, after he came to live in her house, my interest in meeting him waned. In any event, a meeting was discouraged. He had a flat of his own in the downstairs part of the house, adjoining the basement storeroom, which he never left. He did not enjoy visitors, Margery always said, he was impatient and cantankerous. He dribbled and complained. Later, when he was bedridden and increasingly frail, he saw no one at all.

After he died, I was annoyed that I hadn't insisted on meeting him. Now I would never be able to establish a separate sense of him, and Margery's stories would go unchallenged. But this feeling faded.

Although I don't recall the exact circumstances, it was not long after Claude's passing that Margery suggested I take a look through the trunks. Why? Because I am a writer, of course, and it was obvious that the trunks contained a story. I agreed immediately and we made an appointment for a few days' time: she would have to unlock them for me and guide me into their contents. But when I thought the thing through at my leisure, something about it oppressed me and I called to put the arrangement off.

Weeks passed before my conscience pricked me. Margery wanted to get rid of these things one way or another, so that she could find a lodger for the downstairs flat, where the trunks were now being kept, the storeroom having proved too dusty or damp, according to the weather. She wanted to air the rooms and sweep away the shadows of the last months. I phoned and said I would come over to look through the trunks as soon as I had a bit of time, this weekend or the one after. But again, when the day arrived, the same gloomy reluctance beset me and I broke the arrangement. There was a touch of pique in my response, I think: she'd never seen fit to introduce me to the old bugger. Why should I take an interest in his dusty papers? But sometimes, as the weeks turned into months, the very opposite impulse would seize me, as I considered an equally fascinating potential, one that a biographer would appreciate. How much more intriguing it would be to meet the man this way, to gain access to his most personal papers and possessions, without the slightest direct impression of a living, breathing creature to spoil things. Then I would begin to worry that she might have got rid of the trunks in the meantime. I would give her a ring – surely she was getting sick of this by now? – and be relieved to discover they were still there. I'll come past next week, I would say, to open the vault.

At this time, I was making plans to go abroad for an extended period. My departure date drew closer. Finally, Claude's trunks could not be avoided: I would have to look into them or tell Margery once and for all that I wasn't interested. In January 1999, I think it was, I made an arrangement to see the trunks, and stuck to it.

Margery led me downstairs to the flat. It was the only part of the house I had never been in. There was the bed in which Claude had died, covered by a candlewick bedspread through which the quilted lozenges of the bare mattress showed, an empty wardrobe breathing out naphthalene, a shelf containing the eccentric assortment of books he could still tolerate at the end. The four trunks had been pushed against the walls on either side of the bed, the three smaller ones on one side and the largest on the other, beneath the window. Some papers and objects lay on the broad windowsill.

On the bed, resting comfortably against the pillows, lay two stuffed animals, mangy relics of a distant European childhood. He wept when he saw those again, after all the years, Margery said, and told me their names. Nana and the Bear. They were animals of indeterminate species, neither bears nor dogs but something in between.

Together we shuffled through the things on the sill. A tin of China tea, still fragrant after decades in storage, like a flask out of the pyramids. A little calibrated gauge for converting Fahrenheit to Celsius. Photographs, immense enlargements of snapshots, five, ten, twenty copies of the same image.

Meet Claude, she said, picking two or three photos from the pile and handing them to me.

A delicate boy with brown curls, a sweet mouth. This child dressed as a Red Indian, with a nursery-blanket tepee in the background. This child on a rocking horse, with a Roman helmet and a wooden sword.

And Claude again, somewhat older, she said drily, handing me a Technicolor snapshot with a thick white border.

An elderly gentleman, sitting stiffly in a deckchair on some ocean liner, trying without success to recline. The mouth crooked and bitter, the face sharp, a few wisps of hair standing on end in the wind. No trace of the child left, neither the beautiful one with the curls nor any other you could imagine.

After a while, Margery went off to do some chores. Left alone with Claude's personal effects, I felt like an intruder. I retreated to the most public part of the room – the book shelf – where I picked through the titles and made a few notes in a spiral-bound pad about the areas of interest: the occult, boarding-school stories for girls, great naval battles, the American West, unsolved mysteries, infamous crimes.

The trunks unnerved me. I had the feeling that I was on the brink of an obsession, that once I looked inside one of them, I would never be able to turn back. They lay there like an enormous, obvious drug, which it would be wise not to sample. I should refuse them, I should tell her I wanted nothing to do with them.

Nevertheless, I raised the lid of the smallest container, the wooden chest with leather trim. A musty exhalation escaped, as if the chest had just breathed its last. It was packed with papers, letters in coffee-coloured envelopes, photographs in boxes, calendars. Were these Claude's papers or his father's? I had no way of knowing.

The first folder I reached for was full of mementos from sea voyages: itineraries, menus, weather reports, news from the bridge about passages and docking times, certificates issued at the crossing of the equator, featuring a cartoon Neptune with trident raised, sea charts. Here was the plan of a Union-Castle liner in blues and greens, postwar colours that smacked of cocktail lounges and Formica kitchenettes, so crisp you would have thought it had just been printed, with a line of blue ink extending from Cabin 52 on the second-class level out into the sea-blue border, where, on a little raft of blue lines, the following handwritten words floated: Miss van den Broucke.

I came back three times in the next week to look at the trunks, and never got past the surface layer in each one, the thick skin it turned to the world. When I tried to dip below that surface, just to see how deep it was, I couldn't breathe. I had no idea what to do with the trunks, but before I could bite back the words, I found myself proposing to have them carried to my place.

But you're about to go away, Margery said.

That's not a problem. I'll put them in storage, along with my own stuff, until we decide what to do.

A few days later, I came back with the station wagon to fetch the trunks. We got the street guards to carry them out for us. It's not the done thing, distracting them from their duties, but they were only too pleased to earn a bit of extra cash – until they felt how heavy the things were. They were strong young men but they sweated over it, and got their paramilitary uniforms so dirty I felt obliged to double the fee we'd offered.

Besides the trunks, I took Claude's personal library, packed into cardboard boxes. In the end, three trips were needed to carry everything to my house. Nana and the Bear stayed behind. At their age, we agreed, they would not survive the move.

The trunks stood in the spare room. The house, already made uneasy by my impending departure, felt this shapeless new memory in a back room of its mind, a name that would not come to the tongue. A stranger's past was seeping out into the troubled air, dragging the hands of the clock back just when they should have been hurrying forward.

Now that it was done, I could not believe I had brought these things here. In six weeks, I would be leaving (the house had already been let), and I had a mountain of things to sort through and pack up before then. I had gathered the necessary stock of cardboard boxes, garbage bags, mothballs, plastic packaging tape, indelible markers. I had a past of my own to order, and that was what I should have been doing, instead of sitting in this hot, stuffy room – the sash window had been jammed for years: another repair I never got round to – going through Claude's trunks.

On a cursory examination, the contents fell into three categories: books, papers, things.

The books. Most of those in the trunks had belonged to Berti, Margery said. Claude had sold off nearly all his own books when he moved to Somerset Road. Those he'd kept, which had been on the shelf in his flat, were now in five or six separate boxes. In any event, I could tell by the age of the books and the fact that most of them were in German and French that they had belonged to the father. Some of the books for children, the treasures of that unimaginable boy with the sweet mouth and the adorable curls, had his name in the covers. There were some beautiful storybooks, things that could have been collectors' items, had they not been scribbled all over with crayons.

The things. Berti's cut-throat razors. Pillboxes, wallets, portfolios. Twelve pairs of glasses with nearly identical round black rims: every pair Berti ever owned. A broken compass. Cigarette tins with smaller objects rattling around in them (eye teeth, tiepins, a crumbling scarab). Claude's baby shoes. A lock of blond hair in a wax-paper envelope.

The papers. Bundles of letters. Generations of family correspondence (Claude to his mother from boarding school in Manchester, Berti to the family from his many trips abroad). Albums of postcards. Photographs from the turn of the century: hand-tinted, mounted on ivory boards joined by silken ribbons, with tracing paper spread over them like veils. Photographs from mid-century: glossy stacks like playing cards, with thick white borders or deckle edges, a profusion of prints. Forty years of pocket diaries. Schoolbooks, passports, maps, itineraries, stock sheets, calling cards, university notes, newspaper clippings. Death notices edged in black. Wedding invitations, certificates, receipts, bundles of sheet music. A recipe book in black-letter type.

I examined and classified, opened tins and envelopes, and made lists and notes. There were papers in English, French and German.

I had gathered from Margery that Claude was German-speaking, although he'd spent part of his childhood in France and his youth in England. That might be helpful for creating order and I made some notes to that effect. Afterwards, I returned everything as nearly as possible to the place I had found it, as if the disposition of things in the trunks might contain a revealing narrative of its own. But my cataloguing did not disperse the haze of irretrievable significance that hung between me and these things.

It would be better, I knew, not to touch them at all. The custodians of archives and museums wear cotton gloves in the interests of preservation – not of the objects, but themselves. Allowing these memory-laden, use-soiled things to come into contact with living, breathing skin is dangerous. A prophylactic barrier is advised.

In the following weeks, as I began to pack up my household in earnest, I realised that I had misread the message of Claude's trunks. They were more than a warning about a debilitating fascination with the leavings of one life, assembled here in tin and leather and glass; they were a prophecy of the distasteful end that awaits all those who set too much store by the written word. The pointlessness of paper.

Let me be frank: Claude's trunks were not my only burden. I already had Louis Fehler's trommel.

A decade earlier, Louis Fehler (not his real name) had left me his papers to look after while he went abroad, travelling light, and then promptly died. I'd been carrying his blue trommel around with me ever since, packed with outlines of novels, biographical notes and other things, unsure what to make of them.

It's a problem, clearly, that people give me their papers. The reason is obvious: I hoard such enormous quantities of my own. My house looks like a public library or some archive of the ordinary; I cannot get rid of a book or throw away a receipt from Pick n Pay. What difference will another little stack of documents make? I am like an animal lover who gets a reputation for taking in strays. The book lover.

Of course, there's more to it than storage. These papers are *entrusted* to me, placed in my care and assigned as my responsibility. People put their papers, or the papers of their departed loved ones as the case may be, in my hands, because they want me to read them, think about them, edit them or otherwise reorder them, and write about them. They would like me to make something of their leavings.

I tried to explain this to the movers, but they were irritated. The trommel bothered them less than the trunks, which I had failed to include on the inventory for the quotation (they had not yet come into my possession at that time). No matter, they wanted me to unpack the contents of the trunks into smaller boxes. They would injure themselves trying to move these *coffins*, they said, it was unreasonable of me to ask. Finally they relented and said they would move them as they were, but they made it clear they would not be held accountable for any damage done to my property in the process. They fetched a trolley with two wheels and upended the smallest trunk on its scoop. As if to demonstrate that their warnings had been in earnest, on the way out to the truck they dragged the trolley through flower beds, cracked two tiles on the path and knocked a chunk of plaster out of the gatepost.

The trunks were conveyed to a self-storage depot next to the highway near the Gosforth Park toll plaza and stacked along with my own possessions. They looked like ancient sarcophagi among my flimsy boxes. The men were right, not coffers but coffins. Even Louis Fehler's trommel felt insubstantial by comparison. In the stuffy interior of the sealed storage unit, they smelt like old, unwashed bodies.

Why had I taken on these other lives? Did I hope to ballast my own record with others that were weightier, more complete? Their proximity repulsed me.

'We are stories.' It's a notion so simple even a child could understand it. Would that it ended there. But we are stories within stories. Stories within stories within stories. We recede endlessly, framed and reframed, until we are unreadable to ourselves.

When I returned from abroad in a new century, a time to take stock and start afresh, I found a room in a hotel. From there I was able to undo the ravages of my tenants' stay and make some alterations to the outbuildings at my house. At last, after weeks of marshalling painters, cleaners and gardeners, I was ready to move back home. On a Friday morning, I went out to the self-storage depot with the removal men and found my life packed away tidily, a little dusty but otherwise in good repair.

Leaving the trunks in storage was my idea, but the movers seized on it with relief. It was no spur-of-the-moment decision: I had reasoned it through over many months. It would be a good thing, I decided, to keep some distance between myself and Claude's effects, a professional distance. If I moved them back to my house, they would all too easily seem like mere possessions and the impetus to do something about them might be lost. My study was already crammed with redundant paperwork, things I knew it would be interesting to go through – letters, journals, notebooks – if I could only find the time. Better to keep Claude's trunks in a separate place. As soon as I had settled back into my work routine, I would come out regularly to the storage unit and look at them properly and systematically. It might be necessary to draw up a schedule. It would be like going to the office or to the archives to do some research. If my researches revealed that the trunks did indeed contain a story worth telling, I could retrieve them and unpack the material in my study. Before then, I would have the opportunity to sift through it all, setting the important things aside and shedding the dross. Then again, if I came to the conclusion that the material was worthless, inaccessible or uninteresting, I could dispose of it directly, without cluttering up my home.

I did not need an entire storage unit for four trunks. Fortunately, in addition to the full-scale unit I had been leasing (the 'Householder'), the depot also made available half units (the 'Voyager') and quarters (the 'Weekender'). The last was perfect for my purposes.

When the removal men had finished loading my furniture and boxes onto the truck, they moved the trunks into a 'Weekender' unit in a separate block. They did not complain this time: there was a porter's trolley at hand and the walkways between the blocks were flat and evenly paved. Like the full-scale unit, this one had a metal roller door and a fluorescent light, and was equipped with wooden pallets to raise things off the floor to avoid potential water damage. There was more than enough space. The four trunks did not even have to be stacked. Instead, they were set out beside one another, where each one was easy to open. There was room too for Louis Fehler's trommel. It looked quite manageable and contained. I went back home with the sense of a job well done, although in truth the job had not yet started.

What I did carry with me was the half-dozen boxes containing Claude's personal library, which I moved into my study.

The months passed. My plans for the trunks did not work out. In fact, keeping them at the self-storage depot had the opposite effect to the one I anticipated. I was able to forget about them for weeks at a time. Whenever I did think about them, and tried to schedule a 'research trip', Gosforth Park seemed a long way to go.

At the end of the year, when I sat down to look at my budget, I saw that it had cost me R2000 to keep the trunks in storage. I recalled the fact that these same trunks had lain in a warehouse in Cape Town for nearly fifty years and the derisive note I had once made about how Berti and Claude had squandered good money on such a foolish thing. Here I was, struggling to find work, with no money to take a holiday, and doing exactly the same thing. It was high time I cancelled the contract with the depot.

So it was that I spent one weekend of the Christmas break retrieving Claude's stuff. The laden trunks were too heavy to move and the only solution, short of hiring a moving company again, was to unpack their contents into smaller boxes and then move these and the empty trunks separately. With an archivist's precision, each trunk was numbered and each box labelled, so that its contents could be returned to the right trunk, and to the right quadrant and level in each trunk, after the move.

Before that could be done, a decision had to be made about where to store the trunks. They were large, obtrusive things and there simply wasn't room to keep them in my house. Among the recently refurbished outbuildings was a room previously used as a storeroom and tool shed, which I had now provided with a shower and kitchenette and intended to use for guests. For the time being, I decided to pack the trunks into this guest suite. Soon I would decide what to do with the material and find more-convenient places to store it. In the meantime, a guest staying over for a day or two could live with the trunks easily enough.

The empty trunks were carried out to the guest suite and positions found for them. The two metal trunks were stacked in a corner, while the large steamer chest was placed at the foot of the bed as a sort of divan. The wooden chest went under the kitchen sink.

When I repacked the contents of the boxes into the trunks, I did make a few changes. I extracted the more valuable items and put them in a separate carton. More accurately, I extracted the items that appeared to be valuable, the kinds of things a burglar might walk off with – the cut-throat razors, the old tobacco tins, lapel badges, a broken fountain pen, the tin of fifty-year-old tea leaves. Even though these items would have fetched little or nothing on the street, I did not want them stolen, and the guest suite was protected by the flimsiest burglar proofing and had no alarm. These things had only been placed in my care. The 'valuables' went into the linen cupboard inside (where Louis Fehler's trommel had already been stashed). All the rest, the jumble of papers, packets, photographs and books, went back into the trunks.

In my experience, no burglar has ever walked off with a book.

In the following years, I thought often about the trunks and what would become of them. Occasionally, when I went out to the guest suite with an armful of bed linen because I was expecting a house visitor, I would open the trunk at the foot of the bed and stir the layers of papers around. Sometimes I sat down to page through the books and pocket diaries or look at the picture postcards and maps. Usually the dust caught in my throat after a while, and that was a sign to pack everything back in and close the lid.

I thought about the metal trunks too, but not as often. The first time a guest came to stay, these stacked-up trunks were covered with a cloth and crowned with a vase of flowers.

The boxes containing Claude's library were harder to ignore. They were in front of the shelves in my study and they got under my feet nearly every day. To reach my files I had to move the boxes around. I cursed them often. Finally, it occurred to me to stack them in a tower in one corner, but then I had to move them to open the cupboard and the round of shifting and cursing continued.

After a year or two – I think this would have been towards the end of 2003 – I decided to catalogue the personal library. Here was a manageable task, something practical I could accomplish in a defined period of time. Once the books had been listed, there would be no reason to keep them, unless something remarkable turned up. I could take them all to a charity shop or a second-hand dealer and shed some of the burden.

It took me a week or so to type the catalogue into my computer. Each book was listed by author, title, publisher, place of publication and date, and then there was a column for notes on inscriptions, bookplates, illustrations and other distinguishing marks.

As far as distinguishing marks are concerned, I was appalled by the state of Claude's books. The habit of scribbling in books with crayons acquired as a child had clearly never been unlearnt. Practically every one was marked by cigarette burns and food stains, pencil scribbles, smears of ink and ash, gouges and tears. An astonishing range of bits and pieces were trapped between the pages, scraps of newspaper and pictures torn from magazines, moth wings, mandibles, antennae and other insect remains, shreds of dottle and leaves of grass. Some of the papers were stuck with grains of rice and unidentifiable lumps of food. One book contained an entire cigarette pressed flat like a flower. Two pages of another were glued together by a fruit pastille. A chicken bone fell out of *Madame Chrysanthème*. The corners of some pages were folded over and worn down, while others were pierced by hundreds of tiny holes. The books had not only been used, they had been used up, spent, eaten off, walked over, doused, mortified. After ten minutes of leafing through them, I had to wash my hands.

There were two hundred and fifteen books. While most were singletons and some were oddities, a few favoured categories were readily apparent. There were many books on murders and trials – *Famous Trials* by Harry and James Hodge, *More Murders of the Black Museum* by Gordon Honeycombe, *Five Famous Trials* by Maurice Moiseiwitsch; and many more on the mysterious and the occult, including Frank Edwards's *Strange World* – 'Sensational stories of fantastic events . . . astounding and absolutely true!' – and the Reader's Digest's *Mysteries of the Unexplained.* There were outdated works of German scholarship dating back as far as the nineteenth century – Wilhelm Braune's *Althochdeutsches Lesebuch*, Karl Weinhold's *Mittelhochdeutsches Lesebuch* and Sigmund Feist's *Einführung in das Gotische.*

Among a dozen volumes by Angela Brazil, the two that had been read until their spines cracked were *A Harum-Scarum Schoolgirl* and *The Jolliest Term on Record.*

There was a single book by Mrs George de Horne Vaizey. According to the ornate green plate on the flyleaf of *Pixie O'Shaughnessy* it had been a Prize from the Sons of England Patriotic & Benevolent Society Imperial Lodge No 558 Awarded to Cecily Tomlinson for the Best Girl at the Brooklyn School, Dec. 1923. On the opposite page, in the handwriting I had by now discovered was Claude's, stood the phrase: 'galumptious, page 62, line 16'. I typed it into the Notes column in my catalogue.

There was also a single book by Lilian Turner. *The Girl from the Back-blocks* had a Methodist Sunday School bookplate to say that it had been presented to Sylvia Shepperd, Heilbron SS, 27 Nov. 1938. Lilian Turner – the pen name of Mrs F. Lindsay Thompson – was also the author of *Betty the Scribe*, *Peggy the Pilot* and *Three New Chum Girls.* These words at the end of Chapter VIII had been underlined in red pen: 'Joan Darcy, aged fourteen, of Killali Homestead, Killali, Moonagudgerry, away beyond Berribullam, had arrived at Greythorpe School, Miss Sharman's high-class college for young ladies.' I typed these facts into my catalogue too.

But I still did not know what to make of them.

In the inventory of his books, I could trace the outlines of a character, the son of a manufacturers' representative who had become a teacher. I saw this shadowy figure, somewhere between the boy with the curls on his rocking horse and the bald man with the bitter mouth in his deckchair, and sensed his interests, one could say obsessions. He liked women in nylons with seams and little girls with Shirley Temple ringlets and flounced skirts. He was fascinated by automata: he had written several scholarly papers on the symbolism of the mechanical creature in literature. He had an interest in sudden appearances and inexplicable disappearances, in Kaspar Hauser and the *Mary Celeste*, paranormal powers and ghosts. If this man called Claude, a ghost himself, could be given substance, if some flesh could be put on his bones, he might carry the story that still lay in the trunks, scattered among faded photographs, mangled typescripts and postcards in French and German.

How much could he be made to bear though? Among the books that were in a category of their own, the one that bothered me most was *Juden sehen Dich an* by Johann von Leers, an anti-Semitic diatribe by one of Hitler's most poisonous propagandists. Of course, the possession of such an odious book did not necessarily mean that Claude – or Berti – had been a Nazi or an anti-Semite, but the sight of it filled me with disquiet.

I created a folder called Dr T (still wishing to preserve a formal distance between myself and Claude, my subject, if that's what he was) and stored my list in it. Digital records are a marvellous advance on the paper ones in this respect: they gather no dust and they occupy so little space.

The following winter, a pipe burst in the roof of the guest suite and ruined the ceiling and walls. In order to repair and repaint the place, the trunks had to be moved. Fortunately, none of the contents had been damaged. Extracting the valuables a couple of years earlier had created space in all four trunks and this seemed like the right time to repack them more sensibly to lighten my load. I had shuffled through the papers too often still to have qualms about disturbing their arrangement. Finally relinquishing whatever correspondences the physical ordering of the papers may have revealed, I repacked everything and left one of the metal trunks empty. Rusted though it was, the painter was very pleased to have it. When the job was done, he filled it with tins and brushes and took it away on the back of his bakkie.

Then I forgot about the trunks. Margery and I had drifted apart and I no longer expected her to call to find out if I had made up my mind about Claude and Berti. The trunks simply sat there in the guest suite; they had become part of the furniture.

In May of 2008, a thief broke into the guest suite and made off with some linen, a two-plate stove and a handful of ornaments. He ransacked the trunks, throwing books, letters and photographs out on the floor and the bed, but found nothing. This intrusive stranger brought the trunks back into focus for me. I was glad now that I'd thought to move the valuables into the house. Worthless as many of these objects were, a frustrated housebreaker may well have walked off with them. But such a thief was always unlikely to steal papers. As far as I could see, not a single item was missing. But how on earth would I know? One thing was certain: whatever residual logic the ordering of the papers may have retained was now inalterably undone.

I repacked the papers and had the shattered door repaired. I thought about putting in a security gate or an alarm, but the truth is there was not much left to steal out there. My house guests had stopped coming too. The friends who used to call on me felt unsafe in my neighbourhood; they knew people in the northern suburbs who offered them safer, more comfortable lodgings.

After the burglary, I went out to the guest suite more often to check that everything was in order. A few months later, when I opened the door, I noticed a single cufflink lying on the tiles, a silver disk with an ivory cameo inset, perhaps depicting a Roman god. It must have been dropped by the thief, I thought, as he made off with the other one in the pair. But where had he found them? I'd never seen them before. I'd meant to move everything of value from the trunks, but perhaps I'd missed something, some small cache of treasures, a cough-drop tin full of coins, a cigar box holding an old timepiece or an antique razor. More importantly, why had this object, this shiny clue lying in the middle of the floor, remained invisible until now? It seemed impossible that I could have overlooked it. Who or what had carried it out into the open? I checked the windows, but there was no sign of forced entry, as the detectives say. I peered through the keyhole, as if that would tell me something.

In that moment, I wished that the thief had carted away the trunks and left me nothing but this mismatched cufflink. At the same time, the fear of never seeing their contents again ran through me like a paperknife.

So I arrived, by the circuitous and painful route described here, at a point of equilibrium. I had been in possession of Dr T's trunks for more than a decade. I no longer believed I could make anything of them, nor could I imagine getting rid of them. I was simply stuck with them.

It's not true to say I could make nothing of them. Without even trying, I already had. From time to time, when I least expected it, some scrap of the life story of Claude and Berti would drift into my mind, almost like a distant memory of my own childhood. Berti worked as a manufacturers' representative for textile factories in Manchester and he spent half his life travelling. He was always on a boat to Singapore, Calcutta, Yokohama, Colombo, Hong Kong. Among his papers were scores of sample catalogues and price lists, manuals for power looms, tables of weights and measures. His little notebooks were filled with the names of clients, quotations, orders. Wherever he went, he took photographs of himself with the men he met in the course of business, and sometimes with their wives and children, almost as if they were his own. He sent postcards from a hundred different cities, not a few of them now vanished from the atlases – Leopoldville, Lourenço Marques, Port Swettenham, Saigon – always missing Claude, always wishing he were there. The postcards let me imagine Claude too, running downstairs in the mornings in his pyjamas, with a legionnaire's helmet on his head and a six-shooter strapped to his hip, hoping to see a card from Berti lying on the carpet under the slot in the front door. Claude's mother, Berti's wife, must be there too, but I could not picture her at all.

In the autumn of 2011, circumstances compelled me to put my house on the market. The trunks could not be moved again: I would be going to a flat where there simply wasn't space for such bulky things. Even if I kept the papers, as I thought I might, the trunks themselves would have to go, along with the other excess furniture. I had to tidy the place up before the show days began.

The first step was to distribute the contents of the trunks into smaller boxes. I went down to Box It at the Darras Centre and acquired twenty C14 boxes, which the man behind the counter assured me were just right for books. He taught me a valuable lesson about assembling a cardboard box: never fold the flaps over one another (as I had always done). The strength of the box lies in the corrugations that keep them rigid and bending the flaps to interlock them weakens the whole structure. Instead, simply fold the short flaps towards one another, then do the same with the long ones, and run a length of packaging tape along the seam. It looks like a flimsy join, but it's ten times stronger than a folded one.

I did not have time to linger over the books and papers in the guest suite. As quickly as I could, I would almost say frantically, I assembled boxes, filled them and sealed them. On some of them I wrote 'Dr T' and on others 'Claude'. After all these years, the man was out of the coffin and multiplying.

When I was done, there were around a dozen full boxes. Emptied of their weighty contents, the trunks seemed smaller and I had second thoughts about shedding them. All of them were in poor condition, but the metal one would be easy to fix: knock out a few dents, strip off the paint and refinish it, and you would have a perfectly good trommel. The wooden chest could be sanded down and revarnished, and furnished with new hinges and handles. The steamer chest with the hardwood slats was a different matter. Some film-properties company or design studio would love to get their hands on it. It was very *Out of Africa.* I could see it rented out to an advertising agency; or doing duty as a coffee table in the right sort of baronial Bryanston townhouse. You'd want to restore it first, clean it up a bit without making it look good as new, as if it had just been carried off a Union-Castle liner from Southampton.

I did not have the time or the energy for any of this. When I called the Salvation Army to come and take away the furniture, I stacked the trunks in the middle of the floor, ready to go.

The thought of never seeing them again made me sad. I thought of taking a picture with my cellphone. Instead, I fetched a notebook and copied out the labels on the metal trunk, faded yellow rectangles with outmoded typefaces in pale blue and red.

The first read:

TRANSPORTS INTERNATIONAUX
D. FREICHE-PRIM
PARIS

And the second:

SERVICE EXPRESS
M. Thos Cook & Sons
30 Strand Street
Cape Town
PWL 1729 Bertrand T—
D. FREICHE-PRIM
3, RUE ELISA LEMONNIER
PARIS (XIIe)

68, BOULEVARD DES DAMES
MARSEILLE

Weighed against the mass of words the trunks had contained, these few lines seemed hopelessly inadequate. What a useless historian I am! I nearly tore the page from my notebook and threw it away.

The Salvation Army lorry looked like it came from the 1950s. It was not a truck but a lorry. The Salvation Army shield was painted on the side and there was a clattering roller door at the back, which the driver and his helper flung upwards between them to expose a gaping space that smelt of metal and sweat. The space was empty except for some brown hessian sacks and a huge spill of webbing straps like kelp washed up on a beach. The two men appeared to be in period costume to match the lorry: the young one looked like a social worker, fit and healthy, smooth-skinned and crisply dressed in blue jeans and a checked shirt. The older one looked like a survivor, someone who had come through the ranks at the Salvation Army, an old soak who had pulled himself together. He had pitted cheeks and a worn brush of dirty blond hair; the tail of a mermaid, coloured the dirty green favoured in the days before there were tattoo parlours in the malls, showed under the sleeve of his T-shirt. The two of them fell on the furniture with glee. They practically ran it out to the lorry and flung it into the back. They did not bother with the straps or the sacks, as if they had decided there was nothing here that would not withstand a bit more wear and tear. Did they want everything? I asked, suddenly ashamed of my greasy couch and scarred TV trolley. Did people even use such things any more? Yes, they wanted everything, the young man said, they would sort it out themselves. I had no wish to treat them as the garbage-removal men, they should feel free to leave what they didn't want. No, everything, I should leave it to them. A suspicious thought crossed my mind: this stuff will never get to the Salvation Army. They'll drive it to the nearest junk-dealer and exchange it for cash. In an hour from now, they'll be sitting in the Booysens Hotel, drinking beer and eating T-bones. Did they want the trunks? I asked. They weren't in great shape. They could leave them behind if they liked. No, everything, they said. They wanted absolutely everything. It was all good. Good to go.

The trunks went last. The young man took the metal trunk, which was more difficult to handle, and the older man the wooden chest. I followed them to the street, watched as they shoved these things into the lorry, and then the three of us went back for the travelling chest. They hoisted it onto their shoulders and carried it between them out to the street, and I walked behind like the only mourner.

It hardly needs to be said that the relief I felt when the Salvation Army retreated up Blenheim Street was misplaced. I had seen the end of the trunks – but I still had all the papers, packed into thirteen cardboard boxes marked Dr T and Claude.

I still had Louis Fehler's trommel too, but that is another story.

When at last my house was sold, the future of Claude's papers had to be decided. I called Margery, explained the situation to her and asked whether she wanted me to return what was left of Claude and Berti. It was an awkward call. I don't think I'm going to write anything about them, I said. I've tried, really I have. I've picked through these things more often than I can tell you: I know them pretty well. And I just don't know what to do with them. I could invent a character, perhaps. I've seen Claude sometimes, flitting through a corner of my mind in grey flannels and a flecked cardigan, with a book under his arm, I can't see what it is, *Handbuch der Judenfrage* or *The Nicest Girl in the School*, I've seen him. But all these papers don't help. He keeps disappearing behind them. They're crying out for the attention of a historian.

The following week (it was February 2012) I packed the boxes into my car and drove them to Margery's place in Westdene. Her boy Julian was there, twice as tall and broad as I remembered, and he helped us carry the heaviest boxes into the house. Margery hefted a couple too. But I made sure I took only the smallest. I had put my back out with all the packing and shifting of boxes and it had only just begun to heal.

Margery has always had a knack for living well, with a carefree, tumbledown grace you cannot copy from the design magazines. Her home felt open and welcoming. There was a lean-to roof between the house and the outbuildings, and a concrete slab with a table and chairs on it, perfect for eating outside. To one side stood the weightlifting bench where Julian must have done the work of broadening his shoulders. We sat around the table and drank tea. The garden was lush and green in the late summer sunlight. We might have been in the Italian countryside, although there was not a Tuscan folderol to be seen.

A box full of Dr T's effects stood on one of the chairs and I fancied I could smell that compound of musty paper and cigarette smoke he gave off. At home here, I thought.

As we spoke about him, a strange thing happened. I began to see the outlines of his life more clearly than ever. I remembered the crossing to Dover, the garden in Brockley. The little girls on the omnibuses, with their straw hats and ribboned hair, and the striped bathing suits they wore on the strand at Wimereux and Rochebonne. The day on the jetty at Boulogne-sur-Mer when the wind blew Mama's hat into the sea and Berti dived in to save it. What luck he was there to do it – he was so seldom at home. He was always sending postcards from far away, from Montevideo, Nassau, San Francisco. How excited we would get, but Mama would just turn them over with a sigh and stand them up on the mantelpiece.

I told Margery I had binned the books at the SPCA shop in Edenvale and she was relieved. Now that all these things were under her roof again, she remembered certain details: the photographs from Japan, for instance. Was it possible that Berti had led a second life? That he had another family somewhere? We spoke about trying to track down the relatives in Nova Scotia. But they're fish packers, Margery said. What would they do with all this old junk? What could they do that we haven't been able to?

Now that she mentioned them, I also remembered the photographs from Japan. I couldn't recall seeing them on my last repacking of the boxes. Perhaps the thief who broke into the guest suite had walked off with a few things after all. I told her about the burglary and my efforts to keep the contents of the trunks intact over the years. While I was talking, another ghost appeared in the corner of my eye. This time it was Berti, strolling in the gardens of the Nagata Shrine at Kobe with Mr Nakamura. A brusque, self-confident European, with an imperial moustache and a polka-dot bow tie, a man for whom the world was not so much a playground as a marketplace.

It grew late and the air chilled. Julian went to work. Margery fetched a bottle of wine from the fridge and the conversation strayed to other things, the joys and sorrows of growing old, the long years of our friendship, the need to work and the wish to garden. As night fell, I noticed that Claude had left the table, although the box was still there on the chair, mute and unremembering.

Report on a Convention

DAY I

17:30

Pleasantly surprised to see 'Mr Wu' on the board at the airport. Accustomed (almost) to being called Mr Jing. The climate is hot, yeasty, overspiced. No doubt the place would seem filthier without the vegetation, profuse greenery everywhere, enormous leaves and vivid blooms – 'flamboyants' – in which the litter looks floral.

We took the coastal road to the destination, with the sea behind the dunes most of the time, smelt rather than seen. The driver wanted to chat but I shut the partition. As you know, I like to keep my marketing eye open. Papa's face everywhere in the terminal, as expected, on gantries and signposts, and on billboards advertising the Trade Fair along the highway. No sign of bandits.

The Ambassador is one block back from the beachfront – fine views though – within walking distance of the Convention Centre. Or it would be if one could brave the streets, which I am advised against. Rickshaws are recommended. The taximan said I should summon him, day or night, if I want a 'good time'. We'll see about that. Keyed in the number of the control room just in case.

The hotel façade is solid Papa, a gigantic head-and-shoulders, from breakfast terrace to roof garden. A projection with no evident source and very impressive on this scale. One of his best-loved expressions, benevolent and stately, but not overly friendly. Crowned by his unmistakable homburg.

Let me start on the ground floor. The drop zone had a pair of Papas – no handiwork of ours – on either side of the door. Twin commissionaires with the awning resting on their heads, at a scale of 3:1, in ferroconcrete with a marble finish. The airlock lined with smaller versions of the same in alcoves, these from our factory. Gratifying to see our merchandise in situ for the first time. Fixtures, I think, not just hauled out for my arrival. The whole space bathed in red light and that unquestionably for my benefit. It's amazing what they think in these backwaters. I know you find it *sweet*, but you don't have to experience it at first hand. The lobby rosy too, but not as garish, thank God. Ambient, almost certainly chameleonic – sensed it cooling perceptibly as I checked myself in.

A voice message in my earpiece: words of welcome from Mr Booty Khuzwayo, Convenor of the Trade Fair, and an invitation to join him for breakfast in the Parrot Parrot Room tomorrow morning (if I so wish).

Saw my first flesh-and-blood Papa in the elevator on the way up to my room. Not a professional here for the Convention, as you might imagine, but a waiter! He was lugging a tray of cocktails and I held the door. In truth, he resembled Papa only slightly: if there was a likeness at all it was an effect of the homburg and doublet and a certain solicitous, fatherly bearing.

(I remembered your wise counsel, Fei. The eye is the most fallible organ. I'm sure the people here are as various as people anywhere on this green earth and if they all look somewhat alike to me it is the fault of my untutored eye.)

When the waiter got out of the lift on the seventeenth floor, he inclined his head in a regal bow, and I took the costume and the mannerisms – it really did not go much further than that – as an allusive tribute to Papa, who did so much to foster economic and cultural exchange between his people and ours, or a small gesture of gratitude to the delegates at the Fair, of whom I am self-evidently one, for the welcome injection of credit and know-who into the local economy. Unless of course there was something ironic or even facetious in his attitude – a possibility signposted in your helpful briefing papers – and he was registering his displeasure at my presence. I must remember that they do not like foreigners.

Couldn't resist opening the window of my room (know you advised against) to see where I am in the full-face façade. Can you guess? In the bag under an eye! Might have wished to be 'the pupil' . . .

22:45

Just back from dinner. Fascinating outing. Decided to bypass the taximan and summoned a rickshaw with the bedside beeper. 'Rickshaw' is just a manner of speaking. The rickshaw man was nothing like the quaintly costumed porter I expected (we must update our files on the transport sector). He was plainly but elegantly dressed in a leisure suit, silk shirt and loafers; but for some light body armour, discreetly toned to match the suit, he might have been another delegate to the Fair. The only sign of his occupation was a traditional headdress with beaded horns which he discarded as soon as he entered the cab of the buggy.

He took me to an eatery in the neighbouring mixed-use development. Neighbouring being not quite the right word as we had to traverse a dull intermediate zone to get there. I expected rusty shacks, dark alleys and muddy ditches, but instead it was drably uniform, block after block of small, unexceptional houses nestled in extravagant foliage like knick-knacks in packaging material. Almost hyperbolically mundane. Tree ferns and rubber plants with leaves the size of sails. Everything outsize and superabundant.

Must be something in the water. I put my eye close to the glass to make sure I wasn't being hoodwinked by some picture window (don't say I haven't learnt my lesson) but it was definitely real world. People here and there, passing quickly through cones of lamplight, but overall an air of abandonment. I wonder who lives in these catchment areas, as they call them? Then we came to a sector where the pavements were busier although still not crowded, and we passed through an archway into a small square with a tavern where people sat eating and drinking at round tables with lanterns on them, while an orchestra played on a thatched bandstand. The place looked run-down and its patrons poorly dressed, but it seemed welcoming, it had a meagre sort of cheer I found appealing. It made me homesick – so early in the trip! – and I wished the driver would stop, but we bowled straight across the square and out through another archway. I would have opened the window to hear a snatch of the music, but your advice not to breathe too much unprocessed air made me pause, and in any event the driver took no notice of my questions and remarks. I gathered that he spoke the third of the languages and that not very well.

Just as I began to think the fellow was lost, we came into a broad, well-lit avenue that marked the start of the next development. The Cockatoo Cockatoo Grillhouse was in the lobby of a hotel like my own, so much like my own that for a moment I wondered whether we hadn't returned by a circuitous route to the Ambassador. Even the Papas flanking the doorway were the same. I might as well have eaten at my own lodgings – or so I thought until the meal came. It was exceptional. Medallions of protein with the texture of pork, a peppery lime-green rind and a berry sauce, scattered with enormous trumpet-shaped flowers and blood-red petals, the latter edible. Heavenly. (No one will say where the protein comes from. Apparently there are clandestine eateries in the catchment areas where it is served raw, a practice much frowned upon by the authorities.)

Three sightings of Papa during the course of the evening:

– Waiter who brought the protein – homburg and doublet, of course, and the characteristic Papa intonation
– Market vendor – fruit? – glimpsed from the window of the buggy
– Bandleader of the orchestra in the square

Is this average? I expected more.

My guess is that the music was martial and unmelodious. Nothing to go on but the attitudes of the musicians. Much beating of timpani and blowing of horns.

Drank the local digestif after dinner, a viscous liquid flecked with clots of fruit. Felt drowsy immediately. Actually dozed in the buggy on my way back to the hotel. Not myself – you know I like to keep my wits about me.

Hotel where I had dinner (for future reference): The Diplomat!

Another thing: my suspicions about the lobby lighting confirmed. When I arrived back from my outing, I saw that Dutch chap Van den Ende who makes the jumpsuits checking in and would you believe the whole place was bright orange.

Please check for me: scoffeasy; nozzlefruit

To bed now. Mr Booty Khuzwayo is an early riser. I mean to rise even earlier to go through the catalogues, even if the meeting is an informal one. You are quite right to remind me that I am not a tourist but a manufacturers' representative.

Sweet dreams, my dear.

DAY 2

09:00

How much clearer things look after a night's sleep.

When I went down to the lobby this morning there were Papas aplenty! Lounging at the refreshment station, drinking tea on the terrace, going in and out of the Parrot Parrot Room. Three Papas checking in at once.

The impersonators have arrived for the Convention in numbers. Some of them resemble Papa quite strikingly even without the regalia. I thought there must be a few stand-ins among the entertainers, but when I put this to Mr Khuzwayo, he was adamant that there are no professional doubles left. The idea seemed to upset him. He hardly needed to remind me, he said, that Papa left us twenty years ago. It stands to reason that any double who outlived him would be impossibly old by now. All the Papas I saw were no more than stage artists. The Department (of Trade or Forfeit?) was entitled to leverage the heritage product.

Mr Khuzwayo was waiting for me in a booth with two platters of breakfast protein steaming on the table. I took the liberty of ordering for you, he said. We're famous for our protein and I believe you enjoyed your meal last night very much. (!)

And then he squeezed my hand and said: You must call me Booty. Mr is very cold and we are warm people, very warm people. Like our climate. (His hand was in fact hot to the touch – almost as if he were running a fever.)

More surprisingly, he declared his intention to call me Booty as well. Henceforth I am to be 'Booty Wu'. There was something in your notes about familiarity and foreigners, but I cannot remember the details. Is there a protocol there on honorifics? Please take a look when you have a moment.

Naturally, I concealed my bewilderment from Booty Khuzwayo and said I was honoured by his gesture.

An even greater honour awaits you, he said, squeezing my hand again. I am here to invite you to an audience with the King.

The King? I was greatly surprised, as you can imagine, having had no inkling until then that the destination was a monarchy, but of course I said yes immediately. And concealed my further astonishment by lavishing praise on the breakfast protein, which was a little sweet for my taste (swimming in syrup) but undoubtedly tasty.

I waited until the platters had been cleared away, mine still laden despite my best efforts, his wiped clean, and we were sipping a selection of exotic fruit punches from the buffet, before asking: What is the purpose of my meeting with the King?

All in good time, Booty Wu, he said, all in good time.

Business obviously. The meeting is tomorrow evening at the Palace. The existence of which surprised me greatly. I had thought, from your thorough briefing documents, that the only palace in the destination was the Palace of Justice, but apparently we were mistaken. Our information-gathering capacities may have been outpaced by developments. Any further guidance you can offer, diligent Fei, would be welcome. Upload to my memory. I understood that Papa was the Father of the Nation i.e. Democracy. Have I missed something? Time is short, which is why I have paused in my room to file this interim report.

To the Fair!

18:10

Busy day. I trust the orders are reaching you? I can safely say that our merchandise is universally admired. It scarcely needs to be sold. Among the new lines particular interest in salad servers, kitchen thermometers, salt and pepper shakers, kebab skewers, bathroom scales, scatter cushions. Focus on kitchenware as you see. Should be reflected in the orders.

Van den Ende has a new line of Papa leisurewear on a guerrilla-warfare theme. Shoddily made as ever. Not our core business but tempting to make it so, if only to show up the 'competition'. All-weather poncho looks interesting. Have packed sample.

Hardly a spare moment at the stand. Pressure relieved mid-morning by a formal procession of Papas through the exhibition hall on their way to a plenary session of the Convention. A comical profusion, I must say, every shape and size. We exhibitors gathered to applaud.

Gratified to find our merchandise in situ at the Convention Centre: hand driers and soap dispensers in the restrooms. Have noted proposal for small design adjustment to homburg handle. Also doorstop in the exhibitors' canteen. Plaster Papa with arms akimbo. Thus far and no further! Delightful and functional.

Got an intern to watch the stand in the mid-p.m. lull, with strict instructions about pilferers, and slipped up to the second floor to attend a session of the Convention. Interest piqued by 'When Impersonators Intermarry: Type and Taboo' but missed start so caught instead 'The Ethics of Impersonation: A New Approach'. Wordy elaboration on basic dos and don'ts. Very life-like Papa at the lectern. 'It takes more than a hat and doublet.' He had neither.

Sensed animosity between 'professionals' and 'amateurs' in the questions from the floor, especially on the subject of surgery. Some jibing about stand-up versus stand-in which I could not follow. Wish you were here to puzzle it through with me. You know the second of the languages so much better than I do. Sure you might have enjoyed: 'Where are the Mamas? Challenging Patriarchy.'

Meanwhile thanks for the clarification on 'Bhuti'. How silly of me! Now that I know it means 'brother' I shall wear it more comfortably.

23:00

Did I mention that I was going to the theatre? Old-fashioned place but newly constructed, accessed by skywalk. The development has retail, sport, hotel, office and residential components and there's no need to go wandering off into the jungle to take up the leisure offerings.

The story of Papa's life. Few surprises: goatherd, guerrilla, prisoner of state, Father of the Nation. Convincing leading man – but no more convincing in make-up and costume than many an audience member. Papas in every row from the royal gallery to the stalls. His famous victory speech sounded in a hundred voices. They knew it by heart!

Suddenly exhausted. Heard talk over lunch of a sedative in the complimentary nightcap.

Please confirm orders.

DAY 3

23:45

Thank you for your exemplary briefing on the monarchy received this morning. An elected king. Interesting idea. I hoped to quiz *Bhuti* Khuzwayo about it before my audience at the Palace, but our Convenor was nowhere to be seen. This despite the crush in the exhibition hall. Everybody and his brother allowed in today. A pickpocket's paradise. Hardly came up for air, as you will have gathered from the orders, which please confirm.

Forgive me if I skip the day's business and go straight to the Palace. It's a long story, but you must hear it in full.

A limousine came to fetch me at sunset. My hopes of seeing more of the destination dashed by shaded windows. I cannot say where we went, but it was not close by. Drove for more than an hour. Piped music the whole way, military marches and lugubrious hymns, and cocktails on tap, although I did not indulge. Had one only and could barely hold my head up afterwards.

At last, the driver stopped and let me out. I was bearing the nutcracker that you gift-wrapped for just such an occasion, but the driver took it from me. We were in an underground parking garage. He ushered me to an elevator and pressed a button that sent me upwards.

The room I emerged into had the atmosphere of a health spa. Remember that place in Guangdong? Towers of folded towels, potted plants with enormous leaves, pebbles, steam. A young woman in a nursemaid's pinafore and a beaded cap showed me to a cubicle with a shower. When I had freshened up, she said, I should put on the national dress laid out in the cabinet.

I did as I was told.

From what I'd seen of local habits, I expected cotton pants and dashiki, sandals, perhaps a skullcap – or a homburg! – but this is what I found: a linen leisure suit, very finely made, a silk shirt with side pleats, and leather loafers (tan, fringed) that might have been cobbled to fit me – you know the trouble I have with my mismatched feet! There was no mirror to judge the full effect but it felt splendid. My own clothes, which seemed shabby by comparison, I placed in the basket as requested. The nursemaid assured me that they would be returned to the Ambassador – which indeed they were, freshly laundered, along with the nutcracker in its wrapping.

At the nursemaid's invitation, I passed into an antechamber where the servitor who was to accompany me to the audience stood waiting. He took my elbow and steered me towards a wheelchair in the middle of the room. I assured him that I was quite fit for a man of my age, but he insisted that I sit in the chair. Kneeling before me, he lifted my unequal feet onto the footplates and bound my ankles with leather straps. It was done so deftly, I scarcely had time to object, not that I was inclined to do so. When in Rome . . .

Giving my shoulder a reassuring squeeze, my servitor pushed me along a passage to a larger reception area. A dozen men, each clothed like me in a pale linen suit and seated in a wheelchair attended by a servitor, were waiting there. Apparently I was the last guest to arrive, for as soon as we entered a bell rang, a door opened and we proceeded in convoy into the banqueting hall.

The banqueting hall was a circular enclosure with low stone walls and a conical grass roof that reached almost to the ground (there are similar things in the files). In the middle of the hall was an immense radiation pit with iron racks on which slabs of protein were broiling. The servitors positioned the wheelchairs at intervals around the pit and stood ready behind us. I was curious, of course, to make the acquaintance of my dinner companions, but their distant mien no less than the gaps between our chairs did not encourage conversation.

The royal chamberlain, or perhaps he was simply the maître d', welcomed us one and all in the fourth or fifth of the languages. I could not follow much of it, but I gathered from the sprinkling of 'Excellencies' and 'Worships' that I was among ambassadors and judges and other important people. At the end, he bowed deeply towards a shadowy sector of the circle, which I had thought unoccupied, and thus made me aware that the King was already present, reclining on a divan. Just then a golden light sifted down, illuminating the dome of his head and the folds of his silk pyjamas. He looked like a gilded idol in a temple.

It was silent in the hall. Though I craned my neck for a closer view, my companions averted their eyes. The pit smoked and the protein sizzled.

Two stewards came bearing a spatula as long as a dragon-boat oar and a deep-bowled spoon to match. Leaning out over the pit, and propping the spoon on the spatula, they scooped the fatty heart out of the largest slab of protein and held it up before the King. After a moment he stirred and then he slumped forward with his face in the bowl. By the squirming of his shoulders I could tell he was feeding.

There was a murmur around the room. Turning to the man on my left, I greeted him in the first of the languages and then the second, but my servitor took my head firmly in his soft hands and twisted it to face the front.

We sat in silence again with the fragrance of the protein in our nostrils.

At last, the King raised his hand and the spoon was withdrawn.

Figures slipped from the shadows, propped his glazed head against some pillows, and wheeled him swiftly away.

It was our turn to feast. Portions were scooped and carved for us by the stewards and laid in platters on our knees. It was indeed a meal fit for a King and we set upon it like famished beggars, tearing off chunks with our fingers and stuffing our mouths until the juices ran down our chins. A tastier food never crossed my lips. We chewed and snuffled and swooned.

When we had eaten our fill, the servitors mopped our faces with hot scented towels. The familiar digestif was served. Then music and magic tricks – I cannot remember clearly. Then the first of my companions was wheeled away for his audience with the King. Five or six others followed at intervals. The shrinking band left in the hall dozed in the heat from the pit and sipped the liquor. From time to time, a servitor would take a goblet gently from a sleeping hand.

At last, only I remained. Was it an omen? I reminded myself that I had been the last to arrive. Presumably protocols were being observed and I was the least important guest. Or the most? Surely not.

I'm going on, I know. Forgive me. This is the last part.

My turn came. I was wheeled from the banqueting hall. I expected to be brought before the King in an adjoining room, but found myself instead beneath the stars. Yes, my servitor said in a kindly voice, the sparkles I saw above were actual stars. It was refreshingly cool outdoors and the air seemed perfectly breathable. We set off down a path.

The Royal Palace is a vast complex of circular buildings, large and small, linked by catwalks and cowpaths, and serving as bedrooms, nurseries, larders, armouries and refrigeration rooms (my servitor said). It does not have the grandeur of the Palace of the People – how could it! – but it is impressive in its own way. The thatched roofs seem crude to my eye, but are much admired by the locals. As we passed among them in the starlight, I had to admit that they lent a rustic charm to the scene.

We entered one of the smaller huts, my servitor stooping so deeply through the doorway that his chin pressed on my shoulder.

Who should be waiting there under a knuckle-bone chandelier but Bhuti Khuzwayo.

Let's get straight down to business, he said, hooking a stool closer with his toe and laying his feverish hands on mine. At our first meeting his manner had been jovial, but now he was solemn.

He began by acknowledging our long, loyal business association. He thanked me for our ongoing efforts to preserve Papa's legacy, extending his gratitude explicitly to you, Fei, and to all our comrades in the factory, managers and workers alike. Your likenesses, and I quote, are unsurpassed. Instantly recognisable but never literal, always capturing the essence of the man.

We are committed to keeping Papa's memory alive, Bhuti Khuzwayo said (and by 'we' I understood him to mean the government). Every standing order will be filled, no lines will be discontinued without proper consultation. But new values demand new symbols. We have therefore decided to launch a new range of official merchandise in the image of the King.

This was the moment to ask about the monarchy, but Bhuti Khuzwayo's earnestness defied interruption. The fresh air had cleared the fog from my brain and the last few wisps of it now melted away.

When the time is right, we will talk numbers, he said. We have the usual lines in mind – plastic figurines, bronze sentinels, at least one stone colossus. For now, we are simply concerned to establish a likeness. Our experts tell us – and by 'us' I understood him again to mean the government – that there is no substitute for empirical observation, for the eye, Bhuti Wu. Your eye.

Bhuti Khuzwayo raised a finger and the servitor, who had been waiting unremarked, bent over me. I expected him to untie my ankles, but with a few quick movements he strapped my wrists to the arms of the chair. The next moment he was hovering with a bridle. I cried out in panic, but Bhuti Khuzwayo smoothed my hands with his hot palms and brought his lips close to my ear. A small precaution, he said. It won't hurt.

The bridle fitted snugly over my skull. It was not especially uncomfortable, as Bhuti Khuzwayo had promised. I gagged when the bit pressed down my tongue, but the mouthparts were finely wrought and the straps as supple as kid. The earplugs dangling from the headpiece were pushed into my ears. The blinkers lay as soft as petals against my temples.

The servitor squeezed my shoulder and left. Bhuti Khuzwayo pushed me down a cowpath into the audience chamber.

I felt rather than saw the space, since most of it was in shadow and I could scarcely move my head. A round, thatched room even larger than the banqueting hall, unfurnished, with grass mats underfoot.

The King was in the middle on his divan, propped up on brightly coloured cushions, with an amber light sifting down from above. I thought he was wearing a nightcap, but as I rolled closer I saw that it was a golden beret, many sizes too big for him, drooping over his ears like a failed soufflé. Bhuti Khuzwayo parked me beside the divan. Had I been able to move a limb, I might have reached out and poked the King's belly. I gazed at his face, at the bulbous nose, the lemon-peel folds of his cheeks, the melted crescent of his chin, and tried to etch every lump and fissure on my memory. I noted the sleep in the corners of his eyes and the impress of a buckle in the flesh of his jowls. After a while, Bhuti Khuzwayo moved the chair to change my perspective, and by slow degrees, shifting from one vantage point to another, I saw every aspect of the King's head, front, back and sides, and found myself staring once again at his face. My gaze had the weight of a fingertip: three times he opened his heavy-lidded eyes and blinked as if I had prodded him, but gave no sign that he saw me sitting before him.

There is not much more to tell. When Bhuti Khuzwayo judged that I had seen enough, he wheeled me to the reception area and unbound me, and the limousine brought me back to my hotel. Here I am now, wide awake in the small hours. An hour ago, when I sat down to make this report, I was dead on my feet. Now it feels as if I will never shut my eyes again.

DAY 4
06:10

I say I learn my lessons, Fei, but I never do. I have done a foolish thing.

After my report last night, I couldn't sleep. My poor head was swimming with everything that had happened. I decided to go out. Remember the square I saw on my first night here, the tavern with the lanterns and the orchestra? You know me: I wanted to hear the music. I summoned the taximan from the airport, the one who said he knew the destination like the back of his hand, and he agreed to take me there.

We drove through one catchment area after another, avoiding the developments. The streets were even quieter at that late hour, empty but for shadows around a brazier or a man walking quickly with his head down. The colour had drained from everything. I asked the driver to open the window for me, and had to pay him to do it. The smell of cinnamon and standing water came into the cab. A bird call. Or an alarm? I leant my head out in the musty air and watched the dull faces of the houses slip by. Here and there a light burned dimly behind an iron grille. I could not smell the sea.

My taximan was hopeless. All his glowing maps and locators

served only to disorientate him. He took me to squares where there were no taverns and taverns that were not on squares. He found three taverns that were on squares but had no orchestras. He kept pausing to consult his devices and speak to the control room.

At last, I began to feel drowsy. When we stopped at yet another crossroads, I decided it was time to go back. But before I could say so, a man stepped from the shadow of a wall and came up to my window. Papa? No. He was wearing a homburg and doublet, but the likeness ended there. Smiling broadly, without warmth. Perhaps it's someone I met at the Fair, I thought, one of the countless pseudo-Papas, the advertising lookalikes and porn stars, the dregs of the Convention. But what is he doing here? And so shabbily dressed, with his overalls worn through at the knee.

Despite myself, I smiled back. And as I did so, he reached in through the window and took hold of my face. He had big, rough hands, and the broad fingers of a labourer, but his touch was gentle. He cupped my face in his palms, as if I were a child, and tilted my head as though he might kiss my brow. Then his grip tightened. His thumbs pressed into my eye sockets, his forefingers burrowed into my ears, the other fingers sank into my cheeks and probed the flesh below my jaw. He bore back as if he wanted to tear my face from my head.

He would have hauled me out of the cab had the taximan not pressed a button to close the window and lurched forward across the intersection. He clung to me through the gap, and was dragged along beside the vehicle, until his fingers tore loose and he fell away behind us.

The taximan stopped under a lamp and helped me staunch the bleeding. You can imagine how shocked I was. I shouted at the fellow for his stupidity and irresponsibility. But of course the fault is mine. I am the bungler. I would not let him take me to the hospital.

You should see what I look like! One of my eyes is swollen shut.

My jaw is so sore I can hardly speak. I shan't be able to eat for a week. Good thing too. I've had a bellyful of their protein and everything else.

This sleepless night gave me time to think. I wonder if all the travellers' tales about this destination might be true. You know the ones I mean – I must not say too much – that they lie on principle, and eat their young, and fry strangers like us in the streets. I can well imagine it. They keep insisting that they are warm people, but their hearts are cold.

18:30

My dear, what would I do without you? I scalded myself in the shower and used all the staples and patches, as you suggested, and swallowed all the pills and smeared on all the creams, and got through the day's business. No one was any the wiser. Are they used to seeing a face like mine in ruins? Or are they too polite – or dishonest – to say anything? This much our trade has taught me: appearances are everything. I cannot wait to get home. Please make sure Dr Shen can see me first thing on Friday. I need to be scoured, outside and in.

Dead Letter Gallery

Five of Neville Lister's *Dead Letters* were shown on *Alias* at the Galeria Pauza in Kraków in May 2011. This exhibition was curated by Adam Broomberg and Oliver Chanarin under the banner of Photomonth in Kraków.

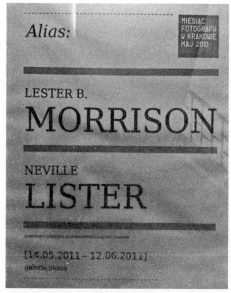

Advertising poster, Kraków, May 2011

Dead Letters exhibition, Kraków, May 2011
(Photograph by Marek Gardulski)

Neville Lister, Paris, 2011

17, rue Boulard, 75014 PARIS Septembre, 1978

Ma chère Maryvomne,

Je suis inquiet à ton sujet! Les nouvelles que nous recevons d'Afrique du Sud ne sont pas bonnes. Dimanche, en revenant de chez Jean-Richard à Auxerre, j'ai vu une chose absolument affreuse à la télévision. Cela m'a tellement bouleversé que j'ai tout de suite appelé J-R, même si nous venions juste de nous quitter. Voir un homme se faire asperger d'essence et être brûle vif et personne pour essayer d'empêcher cela! Tout ça parce qu'il est noir! Ou peut-être y a-t-il une autre raison? Tu dois nous écrire et nous raconter ce qui se passe et surtout ce que tu deviens. J-R et tous les autres àAuxerre se font un sang d'encre.

Ta dernière lettre m'a troublé. Quesignifie cette histoire de déguisement? Je crois comprendre que tu dois te rendre dans des endroits dangereux pour ton travail. Je suis le premier à dire que la recherche est nécessaire. Mais le fait que tu doives te déguiser, t'habiller en homme, et en homme noir de surcroît, me surprend. Te grimer et te travestir, cela doit certainement te créer plus d'ennuis que te protéger? De qui te caches-tu? Et qui sont ces camarades dont tu parles? Il me semble qu'Orlando est à Soweto. J'ai dit à J-R que cela me faisait penser au Roland furieux et il m'a répondu qu'il doutait que, là où tu es, les gens aient entendu parler d'Arioste.

Tu me dis toujours de ne pas parler comme un professeur, mais c'est ce que je suis. Et pour moi, tu seras toujours mon étudiante, même après avoir obtenu ton second doctorat (Mon Dieu, faites que tu l'aies!). Quoi qu'il en soit, parler comme un professeur est l'un des maigres avantages de ma profession, alors voilà: en t'imaginant avec ton visage maquillé de noir (c'est vraiment ce que tu fais? C'est tellement bizarre), cela m'a rappelé l'episode d'Homère oùUlysse se faufile dans Troie, déguisé en esclave. C'est Hélène qui raconte cette histoire à Télémaque lorsqu'il demande des nouvelles de son père. Tu te rappelles? Ulyssesn'y va pas de main morte. Il se roue de coups. Il se fouette le dos jusqu'à ce que le rouge de son sang tache ses haillons saleset se martèle les joues jusqu'à devenir bleu. Puis il entre furtivement dans les rues de la ville ennemie. Son déguisement fonctionne. Excepté Hélène, qui ne dit rien, personne ne le reconnaît.

C'est une histoire remarquable, n'est-ce pas? Mais arrêtons de parler des Anciens. Quand j'aurai de tes nouvelles, je t'écrirai de nouveau pour te dire ce que je veux dire par là. Sois prudente, s'il te plaît. Peut-être que tu devrais songer à revenir à Paris cet été. Maude dit qu'elle peut t'héberger. Ce sera toujours chez toi, ici.

Affectueusement,
Ton professeur et ami qui s'inquiète,

LS

L. Sylvain to Maryvonne Jourdan, Paris, 1978

Neville Lister, Laingsburg, 2011

Okt. 1979

Beste Basil,

Hoe gaan dit daar in die Goudstad? Ek het aanhoudend gebel, maar niemand tel op nie.

Gelede Donderdag het iets onstellends gebeur. Onthou jy ek het gesê ek gaan sodra ek intrek, 'n visdam op die agterplaas grawe? Wel, ek het uiteindelik 'n begin gemaak. 'n Hele jaar het verbygevlieg want ek is heel dag in die winkel. Ek het net begin werk, toe kom mev. Greyling van langsaan en sê ek moenie sommer net gate grawe nie. Ek vra toe hoekom, en sy sê nouja, sekere dinge wat nie genoem kan word nie, lê begrawe in daardie jaart en moet liefs onaangeroer bly.

Ek dog sy skeer die gek maar sy sê nee, dis ernstig, en sy wys my die kaart wat jy geteken het toe jy by P.E. toe is met vakansie en sy moes omsien na jou (d.w.s. my) huis. Sy sê elke X is 'n naamlose ding wat uitgewys moet word ingeval jy iets onaangenaam oorkom, soos bv. 'n ongeluk of 'n verdrinking, en sy agter bly om alles te kyk.

Tans is daar 'n rotstuin wat nie op jou kaart verskyn nie. Daar's skaars plek vir 'n visdam of 'n septiese tenk, wat ook een van die dae herbou sal moet word, nog iets wat jy eintlik onder my aandag moes gebring het voor ek die huis gekoop het. In elk geval, bevestig asb. dat dit veilig is om hier agter te grawe of bel my liewer (jou ou nommer) saans, want dis deesdae beter om niks neer te skryf nie.

Skryf asb. gou terug

Die uwe

M. Benadie

M. Benadie to Basil Liebenberg, Laingsburg, 1979

Neville Lister, Göttingen, 2011

Geiststrasse 7A
3400 Göttingen
Wed., April 13th '77

Dear Norman,

Greetings from Göttingen! I hope this finds you well. I myself have settled in nicely here and am going on well with my work. As you can imagine, there are scholars galore to pore over Kant and Co. but very few with an interest in Netterberg. Indeed, my passion in this direction may be sui generis. It is all to the good: I am left to my own devices and getting ahead by dint of sheer provincialism.

Some weeks ago at the Bahnhof, which is a splendid place dating from the heyday of the railways, I saw something that would have amused you. An old man, a shabby fellow with a brown cordroy hat like a mushroom squashed down on his head, was causing a rumpus on the concourse where the schedules are displayed. He was wandering among the commuters, almost as though he were sedated, I would say, and declaring to no-one in particular, but very distinctly, in well-accented English - "I am the Brain Man of the World!"

I am writing on a different matter though. Please don't think me presumptuous, but when this question arose I immediately thought of consulting you. There is a story attached. My friend Adelheit recently took lodgings with a colleague from the University library. Arrangements of this kind are common here where space is at a premium. When she was cleaning the little refrigeratorin her room, she came across a spool of film in the crisper. Apparently it is common practice to put film in the fridge to keep it "fresh". Her colleague surmises that it was left behind by the previous occupant of the room, a young Argentine who departed suddenly last Autumn after some sort of scandal (she will only say "under a cloud").

The man at the lab tells us that the spool has been exposed. But my question to you is this: How long does film "keep" in the refrigerator? This one has a date written on it by hand which shows that it was taken twenty years ago. Do you think it likely that the pictures are still there? And if so, should one take special precautions with the developing? I hope you are not offended by my writing on such a mundane matter after so long an interval. You of all people will understand, I think, that we are intrigued to discover what is on the negatives and anxious not to spoil them. If they prove to be of interest, I would be happy to share them with you. What do you think?

With my heart-felt thanks (very much in advance!) and warm wishes,

Your old associate,

Karl-Heinz

Karl-Heinz to Norman Ortlepp, Göttingen, 1977

Neville Lister, Amherst, 2011

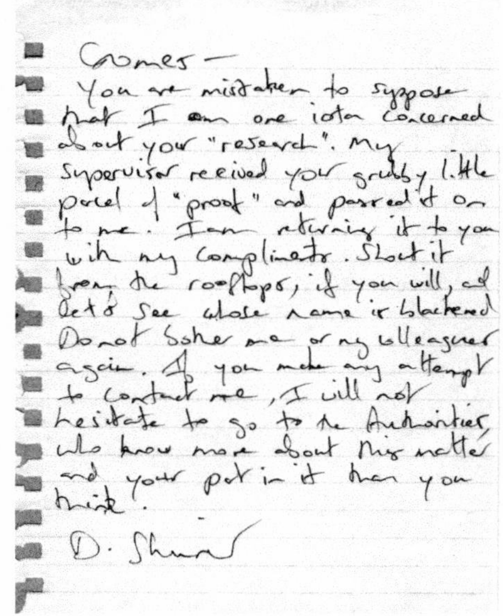

Gomes —

You are mistaken to suppose that I am one iota concerned about your "research". My supervisor received your grubby little parcel of "proof" and passed it on to me. I am returning it to you with my compliments. Shout it from the rooftops, if you will, and let's see whose name is blackened. Do not bother me or my colleagues again. If you make any attempt to contact me, I will not hesitate to go to the Authorities, who know more about this matter and your part in it than you think.

D. Skinner

D. Skinner to A. Gomes, Amherst, *c.* 1981

G.P.-S. 005-0324

G 371

REPUBLIEK VAN SUID-AFRIKA · REPUBLIC OF SOUTH AFRICA

GEVANGENISDIENS • PRISONS SERVICE

VRYLATINGSERTIFIKAAT · RELEASE CERTIFICATE

BEWYS VAN VRYLATING VAN 'N GEVANGENE UIT JOHANNESBURG GEVANGENIS OP
PROOF OF RELEASE OF A PRISONER FROM JOHANNESBURG PRISON ON 80/11/15

1. Naam / Name ██████████ 3429/80B

2. Ras / Race Black

3. Identiteitsnommer / Identity number —

4. Datum van vonnis / Date of sentence 80/11/27

5. Hof en plek van vonnis / Court and place of sentence Hillbrow

6. Misdryf / Crime Bedrog

7. Vonnis / Sentence Ongevonnis

8. (a) *Magtiging / Authority No. — gedateer / dated — is deur die Ontwikkelingsraad te / was issued by the Development Board at

— verleen dat die oud-gevangene na / authorising the ex-prisoner to return to — mag terugkeer.

(b) *Die oud-gevangene is gelas om na / The ex-prisoner was instructed to return to — wat sy tuisdistrik is, terug te keer. / which is his home district.

* Skrap wat nie van toepassing is nie/Delete whichever is not applicable.

B.O./P.T.O.

Prison release form, Johannesburg, 1980

Neville Lister, Queens, 2011

March 12th 80

My dear José –

Received this morning yours of the 8th from La Rochelle which is near Johannesburg I guess. These few lines may give you an idea of how time flew by and answer some of the questions you bombarded me with. Once more I repeat there was nothing untoward about the change in name. Try to see it as it is Brother. This is a new Country where many people come to seize their opportunities. You see your world as it is, but remember that you and I have been moving in two different spheres. When long ago I attempted to get "nat. papers" it was better to be "James" than to be "Tiago" of old. Remember that it was many years ago and the world was a different place. As it is I never did need any such paper since, whether to collect post or get a license or vote. When it comes to mind-their-own-business I am glad I reside in the US of A. As to the "P" it is also a let us say "Brain-wave". There are so many Jimmies here hence the P. It was also a sentimental tie to the time Uncle Pedro ("Peter") came to visit and Mother appointed me guardian over the same. I took a shine to the guy. We sat on a bench at the river eating wallnuts and bread looking at the ducks?! Hardly speaking!!! Benvenuti is a semi-private rooming-house. The owners are from Trinidade and the boarders live up and over the first floor. That is my haunt but I am actually across the Expressway at the actual house, small as it is, with a place to myself in the basement. Underground! I have known them for quite a while and we get along. There are many people from the islands and more everyday. I dare say if I arrived in S. Ozone Park today I would still be Tiago and no problem and you would not say I must be embarrased about the family than which nothing is further from the Truth. I was sure pleased with the pictures you sent and to hear about Óbidos. I can still see the bougainvilia where Mother

Jimmy (James P.) to José Carvalho, Queens, 1980

Deleted Scenes

BEST KEPT ALONE

Sixteen hundred hours, Klopper thought, and wiggled his toes.

'Tell me something, Bate: if these fugu fishes are so poisonous, how come they don't poison themselves? Hey?'

Bate looked at the street. It seemed cold and grey, but that was because the glass was tinted. After a while he said, 'So what's going to happen to this guy?'

'Who?'

'The guy we're waiting for, who the hell else.'

'What do you think?'

'I don't know.'

'We're going to give him a medal.'

'Very funny, Klopper.'

'That's me. Humour in Uniform.'

Bate turned his head slowly until he could see Klopper on the bed from the corner of his eye.

Fugu fish are best kept alone. They are more aggressive to their own species than to other fish. That's what the magazine said. *In Japan,* Fugu rubripes *is farmed for eating. The flesh is best eaten raw but it can also be fried or boiled with vegetables. Fugu fins or testes are good in hot sake.*

ON THE WAY HOME (ROUTE 66)

On the way home we stayed in a motel off the interstate, another ten-dollar dive with red wall-to-wall and woodgrain wallpaper, and the room was so small you could lie on the bed and change the TV channel with your toe. Johnny Carson interviewed a man with a parrot that sang 'I Left My Heart in San Francisco' and it made us laugh until we cried.

We had breakfast in some Denny's or Roxy's the next morning. I remember how noisy it was, how loudly everyone spoke. It used to bother me when I first came to America, but I'd gotten used to it over the years. The waitress brought bacon and biscuits, and eggs over easy with Cheez Whizz sauce on the side, and coffee and cream, and kept up a barrage of questions and comments over the clash of knives and forks. 'I'm sorry!' 'Coming right up.' 'Is that right?' 'Gotcha!' She said, 'You're welcome,' before I could finish saying, 'Thank you.' A reflex, exclamatory patter of pacification.

While the busboy was stacking the plates, he asked: 'Y'all on your way to the Allergy Conference?'

'No, we're just going home,' Mel said with a startled laugh.

'Well, good luck with that!'

WAYFARER (HOBBEMA)

My favourite museum is the one in the Hague. I was very taken with the Hobbemas, until I found a sheet of paper in a plastic box on the wall that said all the figures were put in afterwards. Apparently Hobbema painted his scenes without any people and the Hollanders were quite happy with them like that. But then the paintings were bought and taken away to America, where the new owners had to look at the empty landscapes every day, and it bothered them that everything was so desolate. So they employed other painters to add little figures on the canvases and they thought that 'populating the landscape' and 'humanising the world' made it look kinder and safer. Some of the added-in figures were quite clear, but most of them were so small and hidden I hadn't even noticed them before, to tell the truth. And the painters must have been amateurs because the figures weren't very well done, which is one of the reasons why I didn't realise they were there.

I was happy to get this information, because I am still building up my knowledge of the History of Art, but I must say it spoilt my appreciation of Art for a while. After that, whenever I saw a landscape I had to look under the trees and behind the boulders for someone lurking. I couldn't get lost in the paintings any more. It was like that book *Where's Wally?* (If you've got children – or grandchildren – you'll know what I mean.) Luckily I'm past that phase now. But I can't help thinking that those Americans of yesteryear were wrong. When I find a human being in these pictures, some little wayfarer going along a path through the woods, it's no comfort at all. A terror comes over me that I haven't felt since I was a boy and my heart aches for him, for us.

LOCKED-ROOM MYSTERY

The square outside the window was empty. Along the avenue, the snow lay crisp and even. Scanning that blank sheet for signs of life, Hans Günther Basch remembered the dog-eared Ellery Queen on his bedside table, and thought about the enduring appeal of the locked-room mystery. How often the riddle turned on a footprint or its absence. There were no footprints beneath the window, a single set of footprints led away from the ledge, only two sets of footprints were visible in the snow. A locked-room murder did not always happen behind closed doors, of course. More often than not, it was out in the open and in full sight of the world.

STRIPTEASE

The flight attendant brought me a packet of Supersnacks, which were tiny salted crackers in the shape of stars, boats and clouds, and also miniature pretzels, and mixed in with them a few sweet biscuits decorated with the face of a boy who may have been Tintin, and these childlike bar snacks made me think of the woman and her boots.

What a strange striptease we have to perform in airports these days, taking off our jackets and belts, emptying out our pockets, allowing strangers to frisk and fondle us. At the security check in Mauritius they made a woman put her boots through the X-ray machine. A women's-magazine type, I thought, precise and pointed, in a short black skirt and black stockings, a belt with silver studs low on her hips, a modernist haircut, angular and sculptural. Her stiletto heels gave her that pony-and-trap gait of the fashion models. She unzipped the boots and stepped out of them, and was suddenly small. The stockings turned out to be leggings that ended in mid-calf just below the top of the boots. On her feet she had a pair of low-cut gym socks covered with pink motifs, smiley faces or Pac-Men. Between the leggings and the socks, her pale and naked calves. She padded through the metal detector in the silly socks, while the boots, the leather jacket and everything else went along the conveyor, and of course she looked like a girl who'd been dressing up in her mother's clothes.

STUCK IN THE LIFT

Her application for a higher office had got no response. A week passed without so much as an acknowledgement of receipt. She was on the point of writing again when she got stuck in the lift with four of her colleagues. The compartment had no sooner risen from the 11th floor than it shuddered to a halt and went dark.

Irritated groans and nervous giggles. Then a booming voice asked if everyone was all right.

In those first uneasy moments, she thought about the uses of stories in emergency situations and the storyteller's role as first responder and counsellor. She was familiar with the procedures for securing the area and stabilising the listener, and applying stories in the aftermath of car crashes, suicide bombings and tsunamis, but she had never been on the front line herself and had no ready-made material in her notebook.

This notebook happened to be in her hand. She had taken to carrying it around at work as a sign of her status, much as a medical intern carries a stethoscope. It was a small gesture of rebellion too, a rejection of the paperless-office requirement, a measurable objective in the Environmental Accounting section of the Corporate Balanced Scorecard from which she thought she should be exempt. The notebook held a selection of her best stories, handwritten on unlined paper, the current favourite bookmarked with a silk ribbon. She straightened her spine against the brushed aluminium wall of the compartment and pressed the notebook to her stomach.

After a flurry of phone calls to find out what the problem was and how long it would take to fix, the others began to cancel appointments and rearrange schedules. They had to share three cellphones among four people, and as the devices passed from hand to hand, illuminating one face after another, she tried to place them. The man with the loud voice was the Chief Risk Officer. He was accompanied by two departmental heads, a man and a woman. And then there was an anxious young man in a checked shirt with a red tie plunging through it like an arrow on a graph. A junior knowledge strategist.

It was beautiful, she thought, the play of cellphone light on furrowed brows and pursed lips, every bit as dramatic as a Caravaggio. If only the shrill young man would press the phone to his right ear like the others instead of holding it up to his mouth on his palm like a slice of pizza.

When the first of the cellphones faded out, the Chief Risk Officer spoke again to Maintenance and raised his voice. A mechanical failure, he said after the call. Roll on the day when mechanics is done away with entirely. The words were hardly out of his mouth when the second phone went down. They rationed the last one for twenty minutes, switching it on only to see how much, or rather how little, time had passed, and the knowledge strategist tolled the minutes in a tremulous voice.

Now might be a good time for a story. It took the storyteller a moment to realise that the suggestion was directed at her. The Chief Risk Officer, anticipating the panic when the last light failed, had called for a distraction.

Her stories were neither corporate fictions nor emergency tales, they were simply things she had made up for her own amusement, but there was no time to explain. She opened the notebook at the ribbon. There was a breathless pause. She could not see in the dark, of course, and no one could see that she could not see. She asked for light. The knowledge strategist protested, but the departmental head switched on her cellphone and held the screen over the page.

It was the story of Lamberto Violante, a double-entry bookkeeper in the city of Buenos Aires, who would have led a happy life had he not become terrified of vanishing without trace. For thirty years, he'd devoted every spare moment to avoiding this fate. It was hard work at first, signalling his continued existence and manufacturing evidence that would make him easy to find: he was always jotting down notes, getting himself photographed, leaving messages, scraping and sampling, checking in and touching base. But as the years passed, he became aware that complete strangers were taking care of things, keeping tabs on him and monitoring his every move, and the burden eased. He was able to live a normal life again.

The corporate storyteller began to read.

As the story unwound, the circle drew closer. The arm of the departmental head holding the phone coiled about her waist, the hip of the Chief Risk Officer pressed against her own. She saw the little band of them, huddled around the page like the last people of their tribe at a dying fire. Another tableau from Caravaggio, spoilt only by the red pulse of the low-battery light.

The phone went dead.

The after-image of the page quivered in her mind. All that could be heard was her faltering voice and the breathing of the knowledge strategist. Her eye swept along the lines to where the last words were evaporating. She wondered afterwards what she would have said next, not read but spoken, and almost regretted that she would never know, for just then the lift jerked and the lights came on. As they blinked at one another, colleagues again in the glare, the compartment fell back to the 11th floor and the doors opened.

METAMORPHOSIS

As I left the building, three of the performers came through a side door and walked towards the staff bus. Natalie was not among them. I gathered from their costumes that they had been in the chorus of gigantic insects. They had pulled sweaters on over their black leotards and leggings, but they were still wearing their bug-eye make-up. One of them was clutching an armful of carapaces, which proved to be nothing more than shin pads, breastplates and face masks of the kind used by hockey players.

GRECIAN FOOD

I happened to be in Margery's old neighbourhood when she called about the trunks. I told her where I was – eating a gyro at

Tropical Fast Foods in Langermann Drive – and we joked as usual about their neon sign. 'Grecian Food,' it said. Obviously a cut above the ordinary Greek stuff like moussaka. I said they'd started to put on airs when they moved from Hillbrow to the suburbs. Margery said the only place you'd find Ancient Greece in that joint was in the chip fryer.

Then she told me the news: we were finally rid of Claude and his papers. She'd called an auctioneer, someone who specialises in old photographs and books, and he took everything off her hands for a couple of grand. All of Claude's letters, all of Berti's books. The whole caboodle.

After we rang off, I sat there picking at my cold food. To my surprise, the knowledge that Claude and Berti had finally been dismembered brought tears to my eyes. The leavings of their lives could never be put back together again; all the traces that junk contained of their restless passage through the world had been irrecoverably lost.

RESPONSE TO A CURATOR

From: Pollak Gallery projects [claudiaf@pollak.com]
Sent: Tue 11/16/2010 1:50 PM
To: adam b
Subject: RE: alias show

Dear Adam,

The photographer you're thinking of is Lonni Cadori and I do in fact represent her. She prefers 'lens-based artist' for obvious reasons. Her father took pictures for the cops in the 1980s – there's a news image of him aiming his camera from the back of a Casspir. The idea of shooting at a crime scene is central to her work.

Her ongoing project is called *Over My Dead Body*. Her MO (as she puts it) is risky: 'I visit houses that are up for sale on show days and, while an accomplice distracts the estate agent, I stage photographs in the rooms. Usually this involves planting evidence before making a photographic record. For instance, I might lie on the bed in the master bedroom and leave an imprint of my head on the pillow; or stub out a half-smoked cigarette in a pot plant; or wear a large pair of men's shoes over my own sneakers, make a muddy footprint in the bathroom, and abandon the shoes under the bed.' There is a play on evidence, veracity etc.

I'll Dropbox some images to you in a minute. Let me know if they appeal and we can talk further.

Warmest,
Claudia

Does the name Neville Lister ring a bell? We showed his work here in 2009. A late bloomer, middle-aged, difficult. I'm not sure it would interest you, but I could let you see some new images from a series called *Dead Letters*. Suspicious behaviour of a different order. Just shout.

Claudia Fischhoff | Pollak Gallery
21 Melle Street, Braamfontein 2001
Tue – Fri 10:00 – 17:00 Sat 10:00 – 15:00
If you cannot see the images in this message, click here.

LOST DETECTIVES (51)

Another Meet and Greet, another networking opportunity. He should abscond. At breakfast, he could tell them that he nodded off in front of the TV. He could say he was lost in thought. He could be the lost Detective. But there were so many lost Detectives already. They were all lost.

SWANSONG

A man in short pants and gumboots entered the hall and tottered towards the pit, waving his hands and shouting. I thought this intruder was a drunken dishwasher, but my servitor explained in a whisper that he was a poet sent to keep us awake until dinner was served. One might have expected a poet to rouse his audience by the brilliance of his words, but he relied on the simpler expedient of clapping his hands. He mumbled a few lines, and bellowed a few more, to the delight of my companions, and slapped his palms on his chest and thighs. Once or twice he bent down and drummed on his toes and then clapped both palms to his cheeks with a resounding smack.

Finally he quietened down and pulled a cushion up to the fire. He looked remarkably like the King, only smaller and chubbier, a deflated prototype. He sat there with a trencher propped between knees and belly, smacking his lips.

The poet had a second function, my servitor explained: he was the King's taster. Just then two attendants came with a long-handled fork that had a single tubular prong, and they plunged this into the largest slab of protein on the rack and extracted a sample. This gelatinous rod was extruded on the poet's trencher. With a theatrical flourish, he pinched it between two fingers and displayed it to the assembly. Then he put one end in his mouth. A single bite would have been more than a mouthful, but he hawked it in whole, inch by inch, like a snake consuming a rat, and batted the protruding end with his palm until that too disappeared and his lips were sealed. He chewed, and blew out his cheeks, and chewed again, and sweated and swallowed.

His eyes boggled and he fell back on the cushion. I was greatly alarmed, thinking he was dead. But after a minute, he lifted his head and leered at us, which was a sign for everyone to clap their hands and tuck their bibs into their collars. Then the poet laid his head down on the greasy board and went to sleep.

Acknowledgements

Some of these stories have appeared in *Art South Africa*, *Die Horen*, *Karavan* and *Siècle 21*, and in the anthologies *A Writing Life: Celebrating Nadine Gordimer* (edited by Andries W. Oliphant), *Opbrud* (edited by Chris van Wyk and Vagn Plenge), *Touch* (edited by Karina Szczurek) and *Home Away* (edited by Louis Greenberg). I am grateful to the editors of these publications, to Martha Evans and Sean O'Toole, and especially to Michael Titlestad for his meticulous editing of this volume.

The account of Edward Sheldon's life in 'The Reading' draws on Eric Wollencott Barnes's biography *The Man Who Lived Twice* (Scribner's, New York, 1956), in particular the passage about reading (pp. 169–76). The comments about the 'sewing machine' style are on p. 172; the quote about pity is on p. 167.

The phrase 'translated from the dead' (also in 'The Reading') is drawn from the testimony of Regina Gwayi before the Truth and Reconciliation Commission on 23 April 1996, as reported by Antjie Krog in her book *Country of My Skull* (Random House, Johannesburg, 1998), p. 28. Mrs Gwayi testified about the killing of Sonny Boy Zantsi by a policeman in Guguletu on 16 September 1976.

Neville Lister's *Dead Letters* exhibition was a joint project with David Goldblatt. I am grateful to David for the use of Neville's photographs, and to Adam Broomberg and Oliver Chanarin, the curators of the *Alias* exhibition, for prompting the work. The image of the exhibition in the 'Dead Letter Gallery' is by Marek Gardulski and is used courtesy of the Foundation for Visual Arts, Kraków. My thanks to Natalia Grabowska for sourcing the image.

My thanks also to Minky Schlesinger, Isobel Dixon, Corina van der Spoel, Kim Wallmach, Alan Schlesinger and Hilary Wilson.

I worked on some of these stories during a residency in 2012/13 at the Stellenbosch Institute for Advanced Study (STIAS), which is based in the Wallenberg Research Centre at Stellenbosch University. I am grateful to the Director and staff of the Institute, and to the other fellows, for their support and good company.

Dear readers,

We rely on subscriptions from people like you to tell these other stories – the types of stories most publishers consider too risky to take on.

Our subscribers don't just make the books physically happen. They also help us approach booksellers, because we can demonstrate that our books already have readers and fans. And they give us the security to publish in line with our values, which are collaborative, imaginative and 'shamelessly literary'.

All of our subscribers:

- receive a first-edition copy of each of the books they subscribe to
- are thanked by name at the end of these books
- are warmly invited to contribute to our plans and choice of future books

BECOME A SUBSCRIBER, OR GIVE A SUBSCRIPTION TO A FRIEND

Visit andotherstories.org/subscribe to become part of an alternative approach to publishing.

Subscriptions are:
£20 for two books per year
£35 for four books per year
£50 for six books per year

OTHER WAYS TO GET INVOLVED

If you'd like to know about upcoming events and reading groups (our foreign-language reading groups help us choose books to publish, for example) you can:

- join the mailing list at: andotherstories.org/join-us
- follow us on Twitter: @andothertweets
- join us on Facebook: facebook.com/AndOtherStoriesBooks
- follow our blog: andotherstoriespublishing.tumblr.com

Current & Upcoming Books

01

Juan Pablo Villalobos, *Down the Rabbit Hole*
translated from the Spanish by Rosalind Harvey

02

Clemens Meyer, *All the Lights*
translated from the German by Katy Derbyshire

03

Deborah Levy, *Swimming Home*

04

Iosi Havilio, *Open Door*
translated from the Spanish by Beth Fowler

05

Oleg Zaionchkovsky, *Happiness is Possible*
translated from the Russian by Andrew Bromfield

06

Carlos Gamerro, *The Islands*
translated from the Spanish by Ian Barnett

07

Christoph Simon, *Zbinden's Progress*
translated from the German by Donal McLaughlin

08

Helen DeWitt, *Lightning Rods*

09

Deborah Levy, *Black Vodka: ten stories*

10

Oleg Pavlov, *Captain of the Steppe*
translated from the Russian by Ian Appleby

11

Rodrigo de Souza Leão, *All Dogs are Blue*
translated from the Portuguese by Zoë Perry & Stefan Tobler

12

Juan Pablo Villalobos, *Quesadillas*
translated from the Spanish by Rosalind Harvey

13

Iosi Havilio, *Paradises*
translated from the Spanish by Beth Fowler

14

Ivan Vladislavić, *Double Negative*

15

Benjamin Lytal, *A Map of Tulsa*

16

Ivan Vladislavić, *The Restless Supermarket*

17

Elvira Dones, *Sworn Virgin*
translated from the Italian by Clarissa Botsford

18

Oleg Pavlov, *The Matiushin Case*
translated from the Russian by Andrew Bromfield

19

Paulo Scott, *Nowhere People*
translated from the Portuguese by Daniel Hahn

20

Deborah Levy, *An Amorous Discourse in the Suburbs of Hell*

21

Juan Tomás Ávila Laurel, *By Night the Mountain Burns*
translated from the Spanish by Jethro Soutar

22

SJ Naudé, *The Alphabet of Birds*
translated from the Afrikaans by the author

23

Niyati Keni, *Esperanza Street*

24

Yuri Herrera, *Signs Preceding the End of the World*
translated from the Spanish by Lisa Dillman

25

Carlos Gamerro, *The Adventure of the Busts of Eva Perón*
translated from the Spanish by Ian Barnett

26

Anne Cuneo, *Tregian's Ground: the life and sometimes secret adventures of Francis Tregian, gentleman and musician*
translated from the French by Roland Glasser
and Louise Rogers Lalaurie

27

Angela Readman, *Don't Try This at Home*

28

Ivan Vladislavić, *101 Detectives*

29

Oleg Pavlov, *Requiem for a Soldier*
translated from the Russian by Anna Gunin

30

Haroldo Conti, *Southeaster*
translated from the Spanish by Jon Lindsay Miles

31

Susana Moreira Marques, *Now and at the Hour of Our Death*
translated from the Portuguese by Julia Sanches

32

Lina Wolff, *Bret Easton Ellis and the Other Dogs*
translated from the Swedish by Frank Perry

33

Ivan Vladislavić, *The Folly*

34

Anakana Schofield, *Martin John*

35

Yuri Herrera, *The Transmigration of Bodies*
translated from the Spanish by Lisa Dillman

Ivan Vladislavić is the author of several collections of stories and acclaimed novels including *Double Negative* (And Other Stories, 2013), *The Restless Supermarket* (And Other Stories, 2014) and *The Folly* (And Other Stories, 2015). Vladislavić has written extensively about Johannesburg, where he lives. *Portrait with Keys* (2006) is a sequence of documentary texts about the city. His work has won many awards, including the South African *Sunday Times* Fiction Prize, the Alan Paton Award for non-fiction and Yale University's Windham-Campbell Prize. He is a Distinguished Professor in Creative Writing at the University of the Witwatersrand.